FIRE AND SHADOW

Susan J. McLeod

FIRE AND SHADOW
A Lily Evans Mystery – Book 2

www.susanjmcleod.com

FIRST EDITION trade paperback

Imajin Books - www.imajinbooks.com

October 20, 2012

ISBN: 978-1-926997-83-4

Cover designed by Ryan Doan - www.ryandoan.com

Praise for Fire and Shadow

"A unique fantasy read, engaging and hard to put down." —Robert Kerr, bestselling author of *Completely Restored*

"BEWITCHING! A witch is betrayed. Hunted down for her power, she uses her final moments to cast a lasting spell. A flickering shadow embedded in a portrait holding the key, the Lily Evans saga continues in big way. Susan McLeod has again crafted a hauntingly beautiful tale that delivers all the mystery and mystique her fans have been expecting, and more! If you loved *Soul and Shadow*, you must read this!" —Wendy Potocki, author of *Adduné: The Vampire's Game*

"The characters are interesting and I was kept wondering who would turn out to be the bad one...The book is short and fast-paced...An enjoyable read with a satisfying conclusion. Susan McLeod has done a fine job in reintroducing us to the heroine of her first novel, *Soul and Shadow*." —L.C. Evans, author of *Talented Horsewoman*

"Another haunting, lyrical story from Susan McLeod. Lily Evans continues on her path toward the truth, unlocking mysteries that will leave you breathless and spellbound. A must-read!" —Adriana Ryan, author of *Her Heart's Desire*

To Mom and Dad, with undying love.

Acknowledgements:

Thank you, Andy Griffith, for so many years of joy and happy memories. RIP.

Epilogue

They were coming for her.

She, who burned in the world like a flame, whose beauty drew all men, whose knowledge was so powerful it had to be buried.

How could such a life end in fire as well?

She should have foreseen the danger, yet she had depended on love and laughed in the face of hatred. She'd had time. She'd had her position and her man and her power. The people could whisper and cross themselves as she passed by, but did they not come to her for potions still? Did they not seek help when their families or their animals ailed? Hypocrites and cowards, all of them. Who would speak for her when the unthinkable happened? Who would protect her in her own home? No one.

She was alone. Her husband was away and could not fight for her. She could see the mob approaching the house. Their malice was a palpable entity. The madness in their eyes told her she was doomed. They broke down the door and burst in, Reverend Lacy leading them, quoting scripture while his parishioners chanted and prayed. The loathsome figure of Amos Woodbine wielded his heavy walking stick, his face twisted in triumph. For a moment, rage overcame her fear.

"Lecherous dog! This is how you treat your own family? I swear, you shall not long outlive this abomination." She pointed an accusing finger at the crowd. "And the rest of you—what courage, what character you possess. You bring a rabble against one small woman? How proud you must be of your virtue."

Her dark eyes flashed and she tossed her long, silky hair. More than one male heart stirred. But there could be no stopping the mob now.

"Silence, witch! You have worked your last evil upon this town." The reverend twitched with excitement. "I consign thee to the depths of Hell."

At this signal, everyone threw their torches to the floor. The wood quickly began to burn, aided by the oil in the lamps. She glanced about wildly, seeking escape, but the cowards were blocking the doors and windows from outside. Smoke began to fill the room.

Although it was becoming hard to breathe, she managed a last defiant shout. "Fools! You cannot destroy me. I shall return."

The flames crept closer, hungry for her flesh. She screamed with all her might. Then she crumpled, unconscious, to the floor.

She awoke to darkness.

She was but a shadow now, lost in that dead world, yet not wholly alone. Sometimes she could hear his voice—her husband's—and it brought both joy and anguish. The man she had thought to spend eternity with, their love reduced to memories and whispers.

"Rose? Where are you?" His words were filled with longing and pain. "When shall I see you again?"

But she had no answer to comfort him.

Her only hope was the portrait—her image on canvas, a gift from her husband. Into the painting had gone his love and passion and a spark of the power between them, a spark of her soul. It had been hidden carefully in the attic of the old mansion. The precious book that was the repository of her knowledge was secure as well. She and Jacob had buried it only days before, after that mad preacher had first visited their house. The book had been almost complete, but they had sensed the animosity of the town growing. It had been best to take every precaution to keep the family safe while they made their final plans.

Alas, she had not believed the townspeople would strike so quickly. Jacob had been hunting in the woods with the wolf, and when he returned, he'd found their home a smoldering ruin. Before he could even grasp what had happened, he was dead. Four shots from a townsman's gun finished the murderous business of the day.

But she would not lose him. Somehow she would escape.

Her portrait was discovered twenty-five years later by a new generation occupying the old Woodbine homestead. Struck by its beauty, they hung it on the wall with their other pictures. All were entranced by its magic, but only one had the power to understand it.

Lara, a sickly girl of eleven, gazed often into the dark, painted eyes. Rose reached out and touched her mind, trying to tell her tale. For a time, it seemed that Lara would help. Rose tried to give her strength, but the frail child succumbed to illness, and the family moved away.

Rose's portrait was purchased by a merchant and carried into the next town. Over countless years it passed from owner to owner, until at last it returned to the blighted former home of murderer Amos Woodbine, the identity of its subject long forgotten.

But the spell it cast had not lost its power.

The woman in charge of what was now the Morrisville Museum was unnerved by the painting and loaned it to an art gallery. Rose had waited for so long to find the right connection. Now she could feel it.

Her time was coming.

Chapter One

"You have *got* to be kidding."

I stared hard at my friend Katy. Her fair, elfin face was alive with excitement and her blue eyes sparkled. I sighed. I knew she wouldn't be happy until the druid told our fortunes.

"Come on, Lily." She dragged me towards the tent. "It'll be *fun*. I can't make up my mind whether to go out with McKenzie or not. And you—well, you need all the advice you can get. I'll even pay. What have you got to lose?"

I read the wooden sign with disdain. "*Caliman, High Priest, Sees Through The Veils of Time Into Your Future.*" I scowled. "Yeah, right. His name is probably Joe and he works at Dunkin' Donuts. Katy, really."

"Don't be such a killjoy. I saw Caliman earlier, and he's cute. The only other choice is Madame Rosa, and I don't think she's a real Gypsy. Her jewelry is all wrong."

Before I could argue with such irrefutable logic, a white-robed figure emerged from the tent and watched us approach.

"Look!" Katy smiled. "It's like he sensed our presence. This'll be great!"

I shrugged and gave up. I had let myself be talked into attending the Celtic Faire. Katy, a specialist in Arthurian studies, was in her glory. We had just followed Merlin all the way through Camelot and been seated next to Guinevere at a joust. Unlike every other scholar I knew, Katy did not mind the historical inaccuracies. She simply enjoyed herself.

I had also been having a good time. The fair was colorful, the characters oozed charm, and reality was held cheerfully at bay. The druid was different. The whole fortune shtick made me uneasy, but it would have been rude to back out at that point. Katy had me firmly in tow and Caliman was waiting.

"Ladies," he said when we stood before him. "Have you come to look through time? Be prepared, for such forces are not to be taken lightly." He squinted at me in what seemed like an accusing manner.

Katy was right. He *was* attractive. He had perfect features, with a strong jaw and eyes so clear it was like staring into a blue winter sky. A little shiver went through me. I turned my face away.

"We're ready, Caliman," Katy said. "Show us the secrets of the future."

Oh brother.

The druid nodded. "You may enter."

The inside of the tent had panels painted with oak trees, mistletoe hanging from their boughs. With the sun shut out, the only light came from flickering candles that made the branches seem to move. A carved stump with a rounded top served as a table.

Motioning us into chairs set around it, Caliman sat down and took up a deck of cards. "Here in the sacred grove, we can unlock the mysteries of the universe. The oracle will speak to us through these cards. Hold them in your hands and think about the questions you want answered."

Katy reached out eagerly. I watched, half-amused and half-irritated, as she clutched the cards to her heart and gave them back to Caliman. He laid them out on the table in five rows of five and studied them solemnly.

"I see that you are facing a decision. It seems to involve a man. Should you trust him?" He was silent for a moment. "The cards tell us that if you wish to take the risk, no harm will come of it, and there is a chance it can lead to great happiness." Caliman looked at Katy's smiling face. "Does this make sense to you?"

"Oh yes! What else do they say? I really want to know if the project I'm working on will be a success."

I knew Katy was referring to her long-running mystery novel, a story that featured her university boss, thinly disguised as a medieval woman. It was her dream to have it published someday, and she had finally gotten to the point where it was sufficiently edited and ready for submission.

Caliman turned over another card. "Ah! This symbolizes creativity. This configuration is a very auspicious sign. If you discipline yourself to finish this work on time, you cannot fail."

Katy clapped as if he'd just promised her a Pulitzer Prize.

"But wait. You must be careful. I see a woman who is jealous and would envy your success. I see instability and bitterness, a web of lies and deceit."

"That's right! Webster—she's my boss. She wouldn't be happy if she read my book, that's for sure."

"No, she must not know of your plans. Move as quickly as possible, and all will be well."

As Katy continued to play into Caliman's hands and he continued to make vague pronouncements, my mind started to drift. I was jolted by my friend's voice.

"Lily! Take the cards. It's your turn."

I blinked as the deck was pressed into my palm.

"Think," the druid said. "Concentrate on what you need to know, and the answers will come."

Oh, if only it were that easy. Images flashed through my mind— gray eyes filled with intensity and gentleness, a necklace at the throat of a young Egyptian woman, sand swirling in the desert heat, and my mother, unable to accept the knowledge of what she had done. As if to rid myself of the unwanted memories, I thrust the deck into Caliman's hands.

A startled look came over his face. For a moment, he seemed to be in pain. His fingers trembled a little as he laid out the cards. "There is a storm in your mind. You have traveled a long way to find the blue flower. You hoped it would bring you peace. And so it did, for a while. But the cost was more than you ever imagined."

He hesitated. "Now guilt overshadows your love. You are separated from what you hold most dear. You will go nowhere on this road you have chosen. Once you have met the Other, you cannot escape. Your only hope lies in acceptance. You must listen to the voice within."

He raised his eyes to mine. A spark seemed to fly between us. I couldn't open my mouth, couldn't move.

Katy stared at us. "Lily, isn't that amazing?"

More like terrifying.

I stood up. I had to get out of there. Katy followed me, giving Caliman an explanation I didn't even hear. I strode away from the tent as if it were on fire.

Katy caught up with me by an anachronistic refreshment stand selling fried dough. "Can you believe that, Lily? He really does seem to have some kind of power."

"Katy, that was nothing but nonsense. These people are professionals. They're trained to pick up on every signal you give, and they know their psychology. They're reading you like a book. If they make some inspired guesses, so what? Are you going to remember the ones that were wrong? Of course not. Your mind will filter those out, and only the one or two that come true will stick with you."

I could hear my voice rising. "Honestly, people need to have more common sense. Haven't you ever read Carl Sagan? He talked about the world slipping back into the Dark Ages. Sometimes I wonder."

Katy pursed her lips. "Hmm. I believe I do have a copy of *The Demon-Haunted World*. My favorite chapter is the one about the woman who solved a mystery by re-experiencing an ancient Egyptian woman's life. She had dreams and visions and discovered amazing things. Carl tried his best, but he couldn't quite explain that."

I gave her a distressed look, and Katy's tone softened. "I know how hard the past few months have been for you. You've lived through a gothic novel and still managed to stay sane. I couldn't admire you more. But do you really think it's best to pretend that nothing supernatural ever happened? Answers can't always come from traditional sources. If you want to truly understand your experience, you might have to explore other avenues."

"You mean like Caliman? No thanks. I'm doing exactly what I need to do with Dr. Carson. I'll put my trust in a qualified physician who knows what he's talking about."

"But he *knew*, Lily. Caliman knew about Amisihathor and Kent and your mother."

"Yes, let's not forget my mother. She's struggling for her sanity now, and one of us has to stay grounded in reality. I don't want to hear another word about magic, mysticism, Caliman or Kent."

I blinked back the sudden tears in my eyes. The thought of Kent turned my heart inside out. It had been my choice to separate from the man I loved, but the choice was born of necessity, not desire. He was in England, divided from me not only by miles but also by a whole host of complications.

Katy hugged me. "I'm sorry. We won't talk about it anymore right now. Let's get some fried dough. There's nothing like an authentic Celtic treat to warm the heart and clog the arteries."

"No thanks. I've had enough for one day. I'll wait here for you."

I sat down on a wooden bench while she blended into the long line. I was watching her retreating figure when I was startled by a voice speaking my name. The white-robed Caliman stood in front of me. He had left his air of gravitas in the tent. In fact, he looked very uncomfortable.

He cleared his throat. "I had the feeling I scared you in there. I just wanted to say I'm sorry."

"What's your real name?" I demanded.

He smiled. "Caliman *is* my real name. My parents are big jazz fans and my dad idolizes Caliman Handley. But I just go by Cal. Cal Jones."

"So, Cal," I said in a casual voice, "where did you come up with all that stuff? It certainly sounded impressive. 'Once you have met the Other you cannot escape.' Very dramatic."

He shifted his feet. "Well, it's supposed to be entertaining, you know. People like to hear about themselves. Makes them feel important, and it doesn't do any harm. I don't dwell on anything negative. I don't usually feel…"

"What?"

"Anything so profound."

There was another silence as he struggled for words. "See, I don't just make it all up. I get impressions when I talk to people. Now I'm not saying I see deeply into their souls. But I do get a sense of what they're thinking. Or what they're wishing for. I pick out something positive to tell them. I've never had an experience like *this* before."

He must have realized how much it sounded like a pick-up line, because he blushed. "I'm afraid I sound like an idiot. All I wanted to say was that I didn't mean to scare you. Coming across another sensitive can be quite a shock."

I stood up. "There's no need to worry about me. I don't believe in any of this mumbo-jumbo. I'm not upset. I'm going to meet my friend now. *Goodbye.*"

"So there's no gray-eyed Englishman, no Egyptian ghost, and no mother who causes you so much pain? I'm glad. I wouldn't wish suffering on anyone, especially anyone with a good soul like yours."

"What do you know about my soul?" I spun around and glared at him. "I don't know how you found out about my personal life, but it's none of your business. I want you to leave me alone. Now!"

"Lily, I only know because you told me. How else would I know? I've never met you, and I had no idea you would come here today. I read it all in your thoughts. Your emotions are very powerful. They crackle like live wires. I felt them. I think you know that and it frightened you. I'm sorry."

His sympathy seemed genuine. He was right. I *was* frightened. I had to lay that devil down and be rid of Caliman once and for all.

"If you're actually psychic, prove it. Read my mind right now."

Caliman smiled. "I'm not sure I want to do that. I have a feeling you'll be picturing what I could do with my cards."

I wasn't in any mood for humor. "Come on. I'll concentrate and you tell me what I'm thinking. Or do you need your smoke and mirrors to make it all work?"

"No. I only need a physical link, like the lotus blossom necklace you had."

I froze like a deer in headlights. *How can he possibly know that the jewelry of a girl dead over 3,000 years has forged a bond with me that crosses time and space? A bond I've spent months trying to forget and deny.*

It may have freed Amisihathor, but Caliman was right. It had cost me more than I ever imagined.

He gave me a moment to collect myself. "Would you mind if I took your hand? I don't want to get too personal, but it's standard procedure for readings. I can just use my fingertips if you'd be comfortable with that."

I almost laughed. He was proposing to look into my soul and was worried if a touch would be too personal. Silently, unwilling but unable to stop myself, I reached out. Caliman laid his fingers across mine. A *frisson* went through me, and I closed my eyes.

A memory surfaced, summoned from the depths of my subconscious. I was sitting in an auditorium with my father, watching a high school production of *The Nutcracker*. It was like looking through a door into Fairyland. I was five years old, and the performers seemed like magical creatures from another world. I was captivated by the flowing tutus, the satin slippers, the color and sparkle and grace.

I'd been ballerina crazy for a while. My room had been decorated with every variation on the theme. I would put on my nightgown like Clara and twirl around the house. My father would turn one of the living room lamps on me like a spotlight and announce, "Presenting Miss Lily Evans, the greatest dancer of them all!"

My prized possession was a white and gold box. I could still see it clearly in my mind's eye. All of my precious trinkets had been stored in it—a pearly seashell, a cat's-eye marble, a glittering costume brooch of my mother's. They'd been more valuable to me than any jewels.

As my mind skimmed over the contents, I heard Caliman's voice coming from what seemed a long way away. "I see a jewelry box. It played music and had a pop-up ballerina."

"Yes. I used to wonder what happened to her when I shut the lid. Was she still in there guarding the treasures? Or was she only real when she danced? It didn't seem fair, having to go round and round in circles. Maybe one day she would escape, stretch her legs, throw out her arms and jump into the sky. No more compartments, no more pink velvet, no more lid to hold her down. Just infinite space and the freedom to do whatever she wanted."

My voice cracked. "So I pulled her out to save her, but she broke. Her little legs just dangled and she couldn't dance at all. The magic was gone. I felt guilty and angry because she was so fragile. I put her away in the box and never opened it again. No more ballerina dreams for me. It was all different after that."

I hardly noticed when he took his hand off mine.

Tears ran down my face. "It seems so stupid, doesn't it? She was only a little piece of plastic with a painted face and a tiny scrap of netting for a skirt. It shouldn't have mattered so much. Why did it matter?"

Caliman's voice was very gentle. "Because you were five years old, Lily. She was alive to you. She still is, in a way. You wanted out of the box too. And now you're afraid you're broken. But you're not made of plastic. You're so much stronger than that. Don't stop dancing. Don't let anything make you stop."

As I fumbled in my purse for a tissue, Katy reappeared. She scowled at Caliman. "What's going on?"

"We're just talking," Caliman answered. "I was worried when she left the tent."

"It doesn't look like you've made her feel better. Are you all right, Lily?"

I shook my head. "I don't know. I really don't know."

"Let's go home. I'm sorry I ever brought you here." Katy brandished her fried dough at Caliman like a weapon. "You...beat it!"

"I'm not trying to hurt you, Lily," Caliman said. "I know it isn't easy. I've been through it too. If you want to call me, I'm at the university physics department. You can look me up online."

"Don't hold your breath," Katy said. She took my arm and marched me away. "I'm so sorry. I didn't know he would really scare you. What else did he say?"

"I can't talk about it right now. I need to think, okay?"

"Sure." I could tell my friend was reluctant, but she let the subject drop.

The drive home was mostly silent while I struggled with the emotions raging through me. There was no doubt about it, Caliman's reading had been eerily accurate. He'd known of my psychic experiences and my efforts to try to forget them. For months now, I'd been telling myself that the visions of someone else's past life had somehow been the product of emotional stress. I was encouraged in this belief by my ex-fiancé Stephen and the psychiatrist he had recommended.

Dr. Carson's pills and calm, rational treatment had almost lulled me into seeing his point of view. Since Dame Ursula Allingham—the eccentric archaeologist who had started it all—was back in England, the paranormal was completely out of my life. And so was her grandson, Kent Ashton, the man I loved so much…

"Oh my God!" Katy's shriek and the squealing of brakes jerked me out of my thoughts.

The car swerved off into the middle of the road, which was luckily free of any other traffic.

Stunned, I looked around, wondering what had caused such a panic. I glimpsed some kind of large animal bounding off into the trees. "What *was* that? A deer?"

Katy pulled off to the side, switched on the hazards and sat there, shaking. It was a moment before she could speak. "I-I'm not sure. It could've been a dog, but it seemed…wild, like a wolf."

"There aren't any wolves around here. They live closer to the mountains, downstate. Maybe it was a husky. I hope it's not lost."

Katy let out a slow breath. "I think I lost ten years off my life. It ran right in front of us. Whew! That was close."

"Well, it's a good thing you were paying attention. Nice reflexes there." I unfastened my seatbelt. "I'll drive the rest of the way. You deserve a chance to relax."

Katy hesitated. "Okay, if you're sure. I feel like a bowl of Jell-O." She got out of the car and we exchanged places. "It's really weird though. That thing—whatever it was—was *huge.* And its eyes? I could have sworn they were glowing."

"That was probably a reflection of our lights. Don't worry. It wasn't some kind of beast from beyond." I chuckled.

"That would make a good title for a movie, wouldn't it? *The Beast from Beyond.* Two young, beautiful women whose car goes dead, chased by a drooling creature from Hell, running along a deserted highway—"

"—screaming, twisting our ankles and falling down," I finished. "Been done about a hundred times."

"Excuse me, Lily, but I am a *writer,*" Katy replied. "While it was distracted with eating you, I would bash it with a stone from behind and make a rug out of it."

"I think beasts from beyond are a protected species. You'd be in a lot of trouble, my former best friend."

In spite of our banter, I was relieved when I turned the key and the engine sprang immediately to life. It had ended up being a very unsettling day, and I was glad we were close to home. Soon I'd be back with my own little beast, my beloved Cleocatra, and have time to mull over everything that had happened. All I wanted was some chocolate ice cream and an evening of peace and quiet.

Of course, that was not to be.

Chapter Two

When Katy dropped me off at the Victorian house I rented, a familiar red car was in the driveway. I groaned inwardly. *Stephen. The last person I could talk to about today's happenings.*

My ex had decided that strange events did not take place in his orderly world. The fact that he'd been a part of such events had been swept right under his mental rug. He was just as determined that I forget them too. He was a doctor. He dealt with what he could see and fix. Since he'd saved my life when I was poisoned, I was at the top of his to-do list. I wouldn't be mentioning any druid mind readers to him.

He'd let himself in, which irritated me. That extra key was supposed to be used for emergencies, but Stephen still felt he had the right to do as he pleased. We'd known each other for so many years, ever since he'd become the adored older brother of my neighbor Ellen. He'd gone from adolescent crush to boyfriend to fiancé, but we were both trying to get used to the new role of friend. Setting boundaries wasn't proving to be easy.

He was settled in an armchair with Cleocatra purring on his lap. "Hi, honey. Did you have fun at the fair?"

"Fun" was one of the last words I'd have chosen, considering the turn the day had taken. "It was okay. The costumes were great, and so were the actors. I loved listening to the dulcimer player. Luckily, wandering minstrels make CDs now."

I put down my purse and tried to pick up my cat for a welcoming hug. Without appearing to dig in, her claws somehow remained firmly attached to Stephen's jeans. I gave up and just tickled her under the chin. "I missed you too," I said. Cleo just blinked, and I sat down on the sofa.

"I'm so tired. I feel like I drove a thousand miles. We almost hit a husky on the way back. If Katy hadn't been so quick, we'd be sitting in a ditch somewhere on the thruway."

"You didn't get hurt, did you?" Stephen went immediately into doctor mode. Cleocatra was deposited on the floor, and Stephen began examining my shoulders and neck. "Does this hurt? How about this? Turn your head slowly. Do you feel anything?"

"I'm all right, really. No broken bones, no whiplash. Katy is fine too. It was just scary. It seemed to come out of nowhere and ran straight towards us."

"What would a dog be doing on the thruway?"

"I don't know. I hope it wasn't lost. We sat there for a while, but it didn't come back."

"Were there houses anywhere nearby?"

"No. It was a long, empty stretch of road. Katy thought it was a wolf. She claimed its eyes were glowing red."

"Yeah, well, Katy has quite an imagination. There aren't any wolves around here. It was probably a coyote. They've been spotted in the area. You two are lucky you missed it. That could've been one nasty accident."

I shuddered a little at the memory. "Yes, I know. I feel like I want to lie down for a while. Sorry. Do you mind?"

Stephen looked disappointed, but he couldn't argue. "Of course. That's probably a good idea. Is there anything I can do for you before I leave? You ought to take some ibuprofen to head off any soreness."

"I will. Thanks. Did you come by for anything special? I don't mean to rush you out."

"It's okay. I was just going to tell you about my visit with Brenda. I saw her this morning."

I was instantly on the alert. The mention of my mother had a tendency to do that to me. "How is she? What did she say?"

"She's doing well. She wasn't agitated at all today. We talked about a new book she's reading with her friend Maria. She seemed…happy."

"Mrs. Heinlein's been a real friend to her—not like some of the others. Did Mom mention me?"

"She still thinks you're on a trip." We'd agreed on that strategy when my visits started to upset her. "She read your last letter out loud to me again. She's so proud that you're about to get your degree."

Oh yes, the PhD that's now on indefinite hold because my professor and mentor turned out to be an antiquities thief.

The fall semester had started without me while I'd tried to piece my world back together. However, letters to my mother had to be cheerful and positive so she would think I was safe. She wasn't strong enough yet to face the fact that she'd almost killed her only child just to keep me where she thought I belonged—close to her and married to Stephen.

"Well, maybe I can call her tomorrow. I'll check with Dr. Brooks first. Thank you so much."

"No problem, kid." Stephen gave me a hug. "I'll see you soon, okay?"

"Sure." I kissed him on the cheek, then he left. Cleocatra swished her tail. She adored Stephen and never took kindly to his departure. "Oh, give me a break. It's been a rough day. Can you think about me for once, you furry little monster?"

Cleo meowed.

"I'm going to take a nap. Do you want to come?"

I went into the kitchen for some Advil. In a minute, just to show that it was her own idea, Cleocatra came padding after me. When we lay down on the bed, she curled up in the crook of my arm.

"You know, Cleo," I said as I stroked her, "I'm so sick of this whole mess—having to make phone calls and write letters to my own mother like nothing ever happened, walking around on eggshells while she's in that hospital, never sure of what to do, feeling sad, guilty and *angry*. Everything in my life got turned upside down. I lost...I lost so much." Tears welled in my eyes. "I've tried to be responsible. I've tried to be fair, but Cleo, it's hard. It's just so hard."

Cleocatra's rough pink tongue licked at the wetness on my cheeks. She understood every word I said.

"I met a man today," I continued. "He told me things he couldn't have known. Do you think he was right? Do you think I've stopped dancing? Am I stuck inside the box?"

Cleo rubbed her head against my face. I didn't know what kind of answer that was, but it was comforting anyway.

"It's easy to talk about soaring, but sometimes you have to keep your feet on the ground. I've got to look after Mom. I can't live in England with Kent. I have my degree to finish and my work with Dr. Carson. I don't want a life where dead people's wishes are more important than mine. I'm in control, Cleo. That's what Dr. Carson says. He's really helping me, and the medicine is working, and—"

And the whispers are still there. I just don't listen to them anymore, but they're not going to stop. Once you've met the Other, you cannot escape. Damn Caliman! What gives him the right to come along and start pulling bricks out of my wall?

It was hard enough to keep up a defense as it was.

I shifted restlessly, and Cleocatra protested with a snort. She planted herself on my chest and stared down at me as if trying to bring me back into line. I laughed. "Okay, okay. Enough complaining. We'll just have a nice nap, all right?"

Cleo showed her approval by stretching out beside me and giving a mighty yawn. Somehow she could make herself seem three times her size when it came to crowding me on the bed. I was happy with her company though. Her purring began to relax me until I felt drowsy. My eyes closed and I drifted off to sleep.

I was walking down a forest path with dense green trees on either side. They were so tall they shut out the sunlight, making it hard to see where I was going. I stepped carefully to avoid gnarled roots and the creeping tendrils of vines. I could hear leaves rustling, even though there was no wind. It sounded like humans having a conversation in a language I couldn't understand.

Other than that, there was no sound—no animals scavenging, no insects buzzing, no birds singing. I came to a wooden bridge that stretched across a vast expanse of dark water. I was drawn by an almost irresistible desire to look down into its depths, but when I tried to turn my head, I found it impossible. My eyes stayed locked on a strange white mist I saw forming at the end of the bridge. It seemed to be beckoning me.

I put out my foot to tread upon the planks. At the exact moment I moved, a sudden howl rent the air. In that dead stillness, it was like an explosion. I was petrified with fear, unable to make even the smallest of sounds.

Slowly, right in front of me, a shape began to materialize. It had four legs, a tail and a body covered with thick gray fur. The last thing to appear was the head, with a pair of red, glittering eyes that stared straight into mine.

A wolf! A very large wolf.

"Are you ready?" it asked me.

I knew for certain that the animal was seeing right into my soul. There was no question of lying or pretending I didn't understand it.

Am I ready? Ready to cross the bridge and meet whatever is on the other side?

I looked ahead at the white mist, then back at the wolf. A powerful force seemed to be holding me in place. I couldn't go back through the trees, but I couldn't see what lay before me either. I had to make a decision. I opened my mouth, but no words came out. The answer was still forming in my mind. While I hesitated, the wolf began to fade away.

"You will have to choose," the wolf said, its voice hanging in the air as it disappeared. "Choose..." The last word turned into a howl, still ringing in my ears as I awoke.

Cleocatra was bristling beside me. I hugged her and the howling stopped. "Good girl. It's all right. I'm okay."

My heart was pounding, but whether from fear or excitement, I couldn't be sure. There had been elements of both in the dream, along with a curious sense of expectancy.

I was more than used to strange dreams. In some I had actually experienced episodes of another person's life. Now, with the sleeping pills Dr. Carson had given me, my nights were full of deep slumber without any images I could remember. Maybe that was why everything in that vision stood out so clearly. Even after I got out of bed, went to the bathroom and wandered out to the kitchen to fix a snack, all the details were still sharp.

As I munched on my ham sandwich, I tried to consider possible meanings of the vision, but I was distracted by Cleo. She sat at the foot of my chair, clearly wanting to share the bounty. "I know Stephen fed you. I saw your dirty dish and smelled the tuna fish. Do you want to get so fat that you can't fit through the door anymore?"

She stared at me.

"Ask a stupid question," I murmured. "All right. One little piece of ham and that's it!"

As she gobbled it down, the phone rang in the living room. I went in and picked up the receiver.

"Hi," Katy said. "Just thought I'd check and see how you are doing. Is Stephen still there?"

"No, he didn't stay long. Checked me over for whiplash and trauma and then said to take two Advil and call him in the morning."

"Well, I'm glad he gave you a clean bill of health. He loves any chance to fuss over you."

"I know."

I felt a familiar pang of guilt. It was obvious that Stephen wanted our relationship to pick up where it had left off—when we were still engaged to be married—but so much had happened since then. He had gone away to another state for medical school, I had lost touch with him, and by the time he'd reentered my life, Kent was in it.

Oh, Kent...

"Actually I was more worried about your emotional state—you know, with the whole Caliman episode. I hope he didn't say anything too terrible to you. Are you sure you don't want to talk about it?"

I shook my head, even though she couldn't see me. "Not tonight. I'll tell you later. I'm still feeling funny about a dream I just had."

"Oh, you went to bed early? Sorry I woke you."

"No, it's fine. I was taking a nap and even though I knew I was asleep, it seemed like I was having a vision. You know, like in a trance state. I was trying to cross a bridge and there was a wolf there. Big surprise, huh? I couldn't get past him, but there was something on the other side I felt I had to see. I couldn't tell what it was and my feet wouldn't move. It was such a weird feeling."

I hadn't expected the intensity of Katy's interest. She made me tell her every detail of the dream twice and seemed absolutely delighted.

"Wow! Do you know what you just experienced? A classic transformation dream. It's a beautiful example, complete with all the symbolism."

"What are you talking about?"

"You've tapped into the universal unconscious, all the minds that live or ever have lived, the knowledge and emotion of all mankind!"

"Yes, I've read Carl Jung too, Katy. I suppose the wolf represents my fear. I have to get past it and choose how I'm going to live, right?"

"Oh, it's so much more than that. The wolf is not a symbol of evil. Well, Western culture has made him that way, with Little Red Riding Hood and all. In other folklore, the wolf is seen as a powerful, good figure. In your dream, he's a threshold guardian. You do have to get past him, but he doesn't want to harm you. He just wants to make sure you're ready for the journey."

"Like the guardians at the gates? Hmm." I was intrigued. "They stand in the hall of Osiris when the dead are judged. You have to answer their questions before you can get past them."

"Right. This type of dream is well documented. It's the hero's journey, you know, like Joseph Campbell wrote about? The hero—or heroine, of course—has to embark on a quest, and the first step is having the courage to go."

"I see."

"The guardian can be a mentor too, helping to lead the way. Luke and Obi-Wan Kenobi, King Arthur and Merlin. There are lots of examples in the Arthurian Cycle. But it doesn't necessarily mean you have to go out and save the world. We all make our own journey towards self-understanding and our rightful place in the cosmos. That's heroic in itself."

"So I'm walking through the forest—"

"Representing your old life, the one you'll be leaving behind. Notice how everything is still except for the leaves. They're trying to speak to you, but you can't understand the language. You'll have to get to the other side before you're ready to hear their message."

"And the wolf is the threshold guardian?"

"Yes, and not necessarily the big, bad kind. You know, the Celts worshipped wolves. A she-wolf saved the founders of Rome."

"I know. She nursed Romulus and Remus, the baby twins. That myth actually came down from the Etruscans."

"Uh-huh—the bridge—well, that's obvious. It's connecting your past and future. The dark water is your subconscious mind and all the fears in it. Part of you wants to give in to them, but the stronger part is focusing on the future, the white mist. You can't see what form it will take until you cross the threshold and go over the bridge, but you have to be sure that's what you truly want to do."

"Hmm."

I was silent for a bit, thinking. Katy made it sound so reasonable. She had studied Jung extensively in her field of Arthurian myth and legend.

Am I really at a crossroads in my life, with the ability to move further than I now believe possible?

It was a hopeful thought and a frightening one at the same time, but it did seem as if someone was trying to tell me something. Caliman, the animal on the road, the dream. Clearly something was happening.

How can I just ignore it?

"Well, thanks, Katy. I'm glad you're okay too. And I don't blame you at all for Caliman. I know you meant for the day to distract me. It certainly did turn out to be interesting."

She laughed. "Good word. Hey, don't forget to write down what you dream tonight. A whole pattern could be developing that could help you see where you really want to go."

Of course, I thought after I hung up, *that means no more sleeping pills.*

For a moment I toyed with the idea of not taking them just to see what would happen.

Dr. Carson knows what is best and Stephen agrees with him.

I trusted them both.

Looks like I won't be meeting any more wolves this evening.

After I ate, I switched on my computer and went to the university website. I checked out Caliman's profile and couldn't help but be impressed. He did indeed belong to the physics department and his qualifications were rock solid. I smiled as I remembered my previous quip about Dunkin' Donuts. As odd as it seemed, a leading-edge scientist was spending his spare time dressed as a druid, telling fortunes. Not that I hadn't experienced stranger things in my life.

I turned on the TV to enjoy some mindless relaxation. The first show that appeared was a nature documentary—on wolves. Cleocatra walked right up to the set and started to growl.

"Don't worry." I coaxed her into my lap. "They can't hurt you. They're trapped inside that box, and they can't get out." My mind flashed back to the little plastic ballerina.

Cleo continued to hiss at the screen, so I changed the channel. Familiar music merged with an announcer's voice. "One performance only! Be sure to order your tickets today for City Ballet's *Firebird*!"

Okay. This is taking synchronicity too far.

I clicked off the remote and sat staring into space. I couldn't ignore everything that had happened that day. I knew I'd be calling Caliman the next morning. I had to explore it further.

Chapter Three

I called Caliman the next day. He was easy to locate through the physics department and he didn't seem at all surprised to hear from me. I asked if we could talk, and he set a time for the following afternoon. Now, as I looked across the table, I couldn't help but smile at the change in him. His white robe had been replaced by a white coat over a suit and tie. His curls were severely brushed back, and he had a laptop computer cradled in his arms like a baby.

"I know," he said, reading my expression. "It's quite a switch from druid to doctor, eh? I don't usually get all spiffed up for work, but there was a conference this morning, so I had to look presentable. It's hard enough to be taken seriously as it is."

"Why? I did a little research on you, and your credentials are very impressive. Graduating with honors from the University of Chicago and earning a doctorate in theoretical physics. Wow. Your university profile practically had drool coming off the page."

Caliman laughed. "That's just for show. Inside the department and the scientific community at large, the idea of multiverses is not exactly regarded as mainstream."

"Multiverses? You mean like parallel worlds, string theory and all that?"

"Yes. There are infinite spatial dimensions, where cosmology, physics and philosophy meet. It's utterly fascinating, frustrating and challenging…and fun. I'll tell you one thing. The field is proof that there is so much more out there than we can ever explain. Of course, we never give up hope. Einstein was still working on a grand unified theory on his deathbed. There's always another direction to go in and there's always more to know. Humans are born to explore."

"Are you trying to tell me I'm not crazy, and all of my experiences are just a scientific explanation away?"

"I don't think you're crazy. And I'd like to hear about your experiences, if you don't mind."

So I told him. After months of trying to repress the memories, they unfolded now with crystal clarity. Meeting Dame Ursula at the museum exhibit, being drawn into the ancient mystery she was hoping to solve, falling in love with Ursula's grandson, finding a necklace belonging to a beautiful Egyptian woman, which triggered visions of the Egyptian's life. And most painful of all, realizing my own mother was poisoning me in a desperate attempt to hold on to my love.

Cal drank a cup of coffee and listened, interrupting only to ask the most essential questions. When I was finished, he shook his head in wonder. "Wow. You jumped right into the deep end, didn't you? And you've had no one to help you figure it out. No wonder your mind is in such turmoil."

"I have my psychiatrist, Dr. Carson. I've explained it all to him, and he's been very kind and patient."

"And probably very skeptical." Cal finished my unspoken thought. "What has he done to help you?"

"Well, he explains how drastic changes like meeting Kent and Ursula can be stressful, even if they are exciting. I might've dreamed up all these things about Amisihathor subconsciously just to please them. They're a powerful family and I felt the need to keep up." I stared at the ice in my tea as I swirled it around with a straw.

"I also identified too closely with my subject because I'm an Egyptologist and so in love with my work. My mother saw that I was becoming too involved and was frightened for me. That was what led to her breakdown and her…" I swallowed hard, because it was still so difficult to say. "…to her poisoning me. She thought I would be just sick enough to turn back to Stephen and away from Kent. She thought she was saving me."

"But instead, she almost killed you." Cal put his hand over mine, and I felt an easing of the chaos in my mind, like a warm breeze drifting through a frigid room. "What hell for you, Lily. I'm so sorry. Did the doctor's explanations make sense to you? Did they make you feel better?"

"He says I can get back to normal. All the chemicals that flooded my brain under stress can even out again. With counseling and the right medication, I can see everything clearly. Then I'll be able to make the right decisions."

"Decisions that I'm guessing don't involve any psychic adventures or eccentric families in other countries. Maybe settling down with an upwardly mobile doctor whom your mother adores? He could look after her and give you a nice, safe life. If that would truly make you happy, it'd be fine, but I don't see that in your mind. Tell me, has anyone asked *you* what you really want?"

I paused, thinking. *Have they? Or have they all thought they were doing what* they *thought was right for me?*

"It hasn't been easy to tell what I want. There are so many lives being affected, so much to consider. In a perfect world, Kent and I could be together without these chains holding us back, but that's naïve. There are complications we can't ignore."

"Such as the fact that you're a powerful psychic? Have you been able to ignore that?"

"I-I guess I was just hoping it had run its course and wouldn't come back."

"Like some kind of paranormal flu?" Cal smiled. "It doesn't work that way. Whatever it is and however we get it, it's here to stay. You have to learn to live with it. Running away won't help."

I bit my lip. "How am I supposed to do that? Become a TV psychic? Join a ghost-hunting group? Maybe start a new course at the university— Lily Evans teaches Communing with the Other 101. My academic credibility will soar."

"You're getting a little ahead of yourself. Do you think we go around with neon signs that say 'Psychic'? No! We go about our ordinary lives and practice our craft in our own time. And, like anything else, it does take practice. You can learn to develop it, direct it and even ignore it if you want to. You *do* have some control."

A sigh escaped my lips. "It's been a long time since I've felt I've had *any*."

He squeezed my fingers comfortingly. "You got one hell of an introduction to this. I think you've got a lot of courage and I'm part of a group that will be more than willing to help you."

"Lily!"

I jumped as Stephen's voice sounded in my ear. He was standing by our table with a drink in his hand, looking suspiciously at Cal.

"You never mentioned you were coming here today. I would've met you."

I ignored the overtone of possessiveness. "Stephen, this is Dr. Cal Jones. Cal, this is my friend, Stephen Mallory."

The subtle emphasis on the word "friend" didn't escape Stephen. He said stiffly, "I don't believe I've met you before, Dr. Jones. What department are you in?"

"Physics. I dream up crazy theories for other scientists to make fun of."

I smiled and Cal gave me the barest hint of a wink. "I'd better be getting back to work now. Thanks for the meeting, Lily. I hope we can do it again soon."

As soon as he left, Stephen planted himself in Cal's vacated chair. "Where did you meet that guy? I don't know him."

I was secretly amused at the implication that if Stephen didn't know him, Cal couldn't possibly exist. "He was at the Celtic Faire Katy and I went to last weekend. He's actually a theoretical physicist from Chicago."

"Oh. Theoretical. No wonder we've never met. I deal with *real* issues, like how I'm going to save someone's life." His face was somber.

"What happened? Is it the little Thompson girl?"

Stephen ran his hands through his hair. It was times like this when he looked most vulnerable, and my heart gave a lurch for him. "We haven't been able to stop the internal bleeding. The surgery didn't reveal the source. We'll have to go in again. I just hope she's strong enough."

"Oh, I'm so sorry. Poor little thing."

I had stopped by and given Sandy Thompson a teddy bear one day after hearing Stephen talk about her. She was a beautiful and courageous girl, and Stephen had come to care about her deeply. His genuine concern for all of his patients was a quality some people overlooked in the face of his self-confident attitude, but I knew what a kind heart he had underneath.

"She couldn't be in better hands." I gave his arm a squeeze. "Let me get you something to eat. You can't run on just a cup of coffee."

"You know, a tuna sandwich would be nice."

He started to take out his wallet, but I pushed his hand away. "No, it's my treat. With chips and milk, right?"

"Right." He smiled his thanks, then I got up to take my place in the cafeteria line.

When I returned to our table with the food, I was surprised to see a raven-haired beauty sitting in my chair. She wore a pair of violet scrubs that somehow managed to look better than a designer dress. She was gazing at Stephen with the look of a hungry dog.

"Thanks," he said as I put his sandwich down. "This is Jenny Reed. She's a nurse in pediatrics. Jenny, my friend, Lily Evans."

Jenny's smile dimmed from a hundred watts to ten. "Hi, Lily. Nice to meet you."

"Nice to meet *you*," I said, just as insincerely. I was surprised by the jealousy coursing through my veins. After all, Stephen and I were no longer engaged. We weren't even dating. He was just one of my best friends. I was in love with Kent. *Why in the world should this woman matter to me?*

But somehow she did. I couldn't bear the thought of sitting there and hearing them talk shop, which—in my experience with Stephen's friends—was inevitable. I stood up. "Well, I've got to be going. I'm meeting Katy in half an hour."

"Tell her hi for me. Thanks for lunch."

"Sure." Jenny and I exchanged nods, and I made my escape.

I had a lot to think about as I drove home. *Am I on the right path, trying to get my life back to normal, or is "normal" no longer an option? Can I learn to accept being psychic, if that is indeed the case?* Cal seemed very well adjusted and he said there were many like him. *If they can help me understand, help me learn to control…*

A horn beeped and I realized I was sitting still at a green light. *I'd better learn to control my driving before I worry about anything else.* I made an effort to concentrate as I passed by all the familiar landmarks. But suddenly there came a distraction I could not ignore.

I saw a wolf sitting on the sidewalk, staring at me.

I almost ran into the curb but managed to stop the car just in time. Quickly, I turned onto a side street and sat there, my heart pounding. I looked back and the sidewalk was empty—no kind of animal anywhere in sight.

My mind immediately went into self-defense mode. *It was a dog, of course, and just ran away. Never mind the wild air or the lack of leash or collar.* I'd only caught a glimpse of it, not enough to see for sure. *Another husky probably. Lots of people have huskies. Breathe deeply, Lily. Relax. Be calm.*

After a few minutes I glanced over once again. *Nothing.* The dog had run home, and I needed to do the same.

I steered back onto the main road and drove with my eyes straight in front of me. If an elephant appeared on someone's front lawn, I was going to ignore it. I'd had enough for one day. If there were such things as parallel worlds, I hoped my counterpart was faring better than I.

Cleocatra was sitting on the kitchen table when I arrived back at the house. "You know you're not supposed to be up here. If this is a hint, you can forget it. No more food before dinner for you. Do you want to be one of those fat cats people send around in emails and laugh at?"

Her green eyes bored into mine. *You will obey my will. Submit to my power. I want a treat. You will give me a treat.*

"Well, I guess one won't hurt." I took a treat out of the package and gave it to her. She jumped down and followed me into the next room to curl up beside me on the sofa.

"It's been quite a day, Cleo. I met with Cal first. He really is nice. I felt better after I talked to him. He makes all the things that have happened to me seem—well, not normal exactly, but not freakish either. He says he can help me develop and learn to control my…powers? No, that makes me sound like Supergirl. Gifts? Maybe. Although sometimes they seem a lot more of a curse. Oh, I don't know."

I scratched behind her ears as she purred. "It's all very confusing, but it's nice to know there are choices. And guess what happened next? Your precious Stephen showed up. So did a woman who looked like she wanted to eat him for lunch. He obviously likes women with dark hair."

Cleocatra stopped purring and climbed over me to go and sit on the other side of the sofa.

"I'm sorry," I said. "I'm sure he'll always love you best."

She ignored me and began batting at the phone on the end table.

I reached to stop her before she knocked the receiver out of its cradle. "Are you expecting a call? I'll be glad to get it for you. Come on now. Stop that!"

All of a sudden the phone began to ring.

"Cleo, you scare me sometimes," I murmured as I picked it up.

"Hey. It's me. How did your meeting with Cal go?"

"I was just telling Cleo all about it," I answered Katy. "It went very well. I like him. He makes me feel better, safer. We've got a lot more to talk about, but it was a good start."

"I'm glad he's helping you. What does Cleo say?"

I looked at my pet and laughed. "She's too busy being jealous right now to spare a thought for Cal. Stephen has been seen with another woman."

"Are you joking? What woman?"

"A nurse who works in pediatrics with him—a beautiful brunette named Jenny. They were having lunch together in the cafeteria. Cleo does not approve at all."

"And what about you? How does it make *you* feel?"

"Well, how should I feel? Stephen understands we're just friends. He's been a huge support to me, and I wish him happiness with whomever he chooses."

"*Okay.* So what is she like?"

"I can't judge after two or three minutes, but I'd say pretty full of herself, with the instincts of a barracuda."

"Uh-huh. I'm glad you can remain unbiased. Your selfless devotion to your friends is one of your best qualities. It's nice that you've been able to maintain it."

"Thank you, Katy. It's poor Cleo I worry about. We did pick her out together, and she thinks of him as a father. I don't want him spending all of his time with this Jenny and becoming a deadbeat dad. What if..." I lowered my voice to a whisper. "...she has a D-O-G?"

Cleocatra screeched.

"I told you she can spell. Stop doing that."

"Oh sweetheart, I'm sorry." I stroked the cat's ruffled fur. "I was only joking. I promise, not another word about it."

Cleo left the room with what could only be described as a withering look.

I sighed. "All right, I admit it was a little strange seeing another woman eye Stephen, but it's bound to happen. After all, he's a handsome man and a confident, successful one too. I don't expect him to spend all his time hanging around with me."

"It has been nice, though, hasn't it? To know he's there, that he cares so much, that you can count on him. It's a luxury most women can only dream about."

"Are you suggesting I'm leading him on?" I was hurt. "I'd never do that. He knows exactly how I feel, and he still wants to be friends."

"Lily, I know you'd never do it on purpose. I don't think even *you* know exactly how you feel. Kent's a long way from here, but you see Stephen almost every day. It's got to be confusing, what with everything you've been through. All I'm saying is that I don't want you to get hurt. You've got to realize that time isn't standing still for other people. Don't let it blindside you when things like this happen."

"Do you think Kent is dating someone else?" I demanded. "He wouldn't, not without telling me. He agreed to wait while things get sorted out, he understands—"

"Whoa there, Nellie! No, I'm not saying Kent is dating anyone else. I'm not trying to scare you. I just want you to focus. Understanding yourself is the key. Everything else follows. I think talking to Cal is a very brave step. Tell me more about what happened."

Still a bit hurt, I described the meeting.

"Well, he sounds nice," Katy said when I'd finished. "And these others? Are you going to get their advice too?"

"Yes. I want to see how different people handle it. I hope Cal introduces us soon."

"Good. You're doing just what you need to do. And don't forget to tell them about your dream."

"Is this really crossing the bridge to a new life?"

"I think so and it's going to be built on your strengths. You're going to do it, Lily."

Mollified, I hung up the phone feeling more optimistic. *Maybe I will finally get some answers.*

Chapter Four

Wednesday I had to go downtown to run some errands. I parked on University Avenue, right outside one of my favorite bakeries. *I will treat myself first,* I decided.

It was another glorious October day with clear blue skies. The sun had lost its summer heat but acquired a mellow glow. It was always a pleasure to walk down that street so close to the museum, with mosaic in the pavement and sculptures outside the buildings. I always smiled at the giant pencil in front of the bookstore and the whimsical blue cat curled up on a decorated bench. Appropriately, it flanked the store I was headed for first, Kit-N-Kaboodle.

Ever since tasting her first treat from there, Cleocatra had craved them above all else. *Grocery store toys or catnip for a feline descended from sacred Egyptian animals? You must be joking.*

So I bought her a bottle of treats, some fish, a can of salmon and a squeaky mouse with organic catnip to replace the one she'd torn to shreds.

On my way to the checkout, I passed a woman who had a white Angora tucked into a baby carrier slung over her shoulder. *I'll never get that bad*, I vowed to myself as I put my expensive purchases on the counter.

Next I went into the academic bookstore and browsed in the ancient history section. My shelves already groaned beneath the weight of all my volumes, but there was always a new and exciting book about Egypt coming out. This time I found two and wrote down the titles. My birthday was at the end of the month, and I hoped maybe those works would find their way into my hands.

I visited the post office and the bank, then stopped in the small gallery that displayed my work, just to see how things were going. I wanted to check the inventory and look at my pictures, to remind myself that I could indeed paint.

My art had suffered as of late, but I decided it was a small price to pay for some peace of mind. Too much imagination had helped feed my troubles, after all. I knew when I was completely stable, my creativity would come back and be firmly under my control.

Carolyn, the owner, was nowhere to be seen. There was one customer browsing around, unfortunately nowhere near my section. She was staring at a picture so intently that it aroused my curiosity. In fact, she seemed transfixed by it.

A little surge of jealousy went through me. *Why can't she look at my work that way?* I stood for a while, hoping she might wander over, but she didn't. *Oh well. To each their own.* Two of my Egyptian watercolors were gone, one of Hatshepsut's temple and one of cranes flying over the Nile. That left three offerings. *I'd better bring some more in soon.* Heaven knew I needed the money, especially after splurging on Cleo.

"Lily."

I turned as Carolyn came walking into the room with a welcoming smile. Everything seemed to light up when that smile appeared. It radiated warmth and sweetness. Carolyn was one of the nicest people I knew.

"It's so good to see you again." She gave me a hug. "And how lucky that you came today. I was just writing up a sales slip in the back. Isis has found a new home. A very discerning gentleman was in a bit earlier, and he picked her right out. Do you want to say goodbye?"

I lifted the picture of the goddess off of its easel. It hadn't been easy for me to part with it, but Isis was always a popular subject. I gave her a last look and handed her over to Carolyn. "I hate to see her go, but I love the idea of eating more," I said, only half-joking.

"At the rate you're going, you'll soon be all right. You're a very talented artist, Lily. That's a wonderful skill to have as a backup. When you get school sorted out and land a job, there'll be no stopping you."

"Carolyn, I should make you my manager. I'm so grateful for all your help."

"It's my pleasure. Now let me go wrap this up. I'll need others to fill these empty spaces too."

"I'll bring more in, I promise," I said as she bustled away.

I went over to see the mystery picture. The customer looking at it had run like a startled rabbit at Carolyn's entrance, slamming the door behind her. I wanted to see the painting she'd found so enthralling.

It was a portrait of a woman dressed in seventeenth-century clothing. Tight black curls were piled up on her head, and more cascaded down her bare shoulders. Her gown was pink, her skin was white, and she had a lovely face with high cheekbones.

Her most striking feature was her large brown eyes. They stared out across the years as if their owner were looking right through me. It was eerie, and I wanted to turn away and hide myself from her gaze. There was something in those eyes, a kind of voracious hunger. I wasn't sure what to call it, but it frightened me. Still, I couldn't stop staring at her. She was so...alive.

Slowly, against my will, I reached out and ran my fingers over her painted features. All at once, I could hear people shouting, chanting and screaming. Smoke was filling my nostrils and my lungs. Flames were rising all around me, the heat becoming more and more unbearable. Still, a voice was crying defiantly. "Fools! You cannot destroy me. I shall return!"

"Lily!"

I jumped as Carolyn said my name. She was standing beside me again, looking puzzled.

"I've had to call you three times. Your painting is ready to go."

I answered her unspoken question. "This is quite a portrait, Carolyn. It's hard to look away. Who's the artist?"

"That's an interesting question. It's on loan from the Morrisville Museum. There's no signature, and I don't recognize any artist or style. I've done some research, but I haven't turned up anything. It's old though. It could actually be from the seventeenth century. Isn't it fascinating?"

"It's a beautiful portrait," I agreed, "but she's almost...well, *too* alive."

"I know what you mean. She's been here for three days, and everyone who comes in is drawn to her like a magnet. But no one asks who she is or whether she's for sale. Sometimes I swear people are frightened of her."

I'll bet they are. "It's probably the eyes. They seem to be looking right at me. She'd be perfect in a haunted house."

"Wouldn't she though? Well, my dear, here is your check. Don't forget to bring me more work. Yours has such a gentle and spiritual quality to it, not like the witch."

"The witch?" I asked, startled.

"That's what I call her. She does seem to cast a spell over people."

"Well, good luck with her. I'll come in again at the end of the week, okay? And thanks again."

"Thank you, Lily. I'll see you later."

I walked back to my car, struggling with conflicting emotions. I was glad my pictures were selling and delighted to have the money, but the experience with the portrait had unsettled me. *If the woman had been considered a witch, did I just hear echoes of her execution? Was she burned at the stake?*

It was a horrible thing to contemplate, and I didn't want to. I tried hard to push it out of my mind. I went into the bakery and bought some brownies. Chocolate was a powerful protector. "Don't bother," I told the girl as she started to tape the box shut, and we both laughed.

"That kind of day?" the clerk asked.

"Yes, that kind of day. Thanks."

I ate one sitting on a bench outside the door, then brushed away the crumbs and got into my car. As I prepared to leave, I checked the rearview mirror. A pair of brown eyes stared back at me. I froze in horror, not even able to breathe. Then, just as suddenly, they were gone.

I sat there for a full two minutes, not moving. Only the *toot* of a horn brought me out of my shock. Someone was waiting impatiently for the parking space. Still shaken, I pulled into the road. *Lily, Lily,* I told myself firmly, steering with an effort. *It was just your imagination. Breathe. Concentrate. Drive.*

I was home before I even realized it. I walked in, shut the door and stood looking at my familiar and comfortable living room. *You're safe. Don't worry. You're safe.*

Cleocatra came in, and I scooped her up into my arms. "It was that portrait, Cleo. It must be of a witch. The eyes—they creep everyone out. Carolyn said so."

I nuzzled her soft fur. "It's all right," I crooned, as if she were the one who needed reassurance. "This is all Cal's fault. He got me started back on this road, and Katy with her transformation dreams. I need one of my pills." I set Cleo down and went into the kitchen. I poured a glass of milk and took a bottle out of the cabinet.

As I was swallowing, Cleo followed and stood looking at me as if to say, *Well? Are you the only one who gets refreshment around here?*

Already feeling better, I rummaged in the bag and produced her treats. "Here you go, sweetheart. Have two. And I'll eat another brownie. After all, Isis found a new home today, and we have to celebrate."

Cleo was in complete agreement. I cut the tag off her mouse and tossed it on the floor in front of her. She sniffed at it, smelled the catnip and pounced on it immediately. After batting it about with her paws, she grasped it firmly, rolled over with it a few times and started to chew.

I laughed at her antics, which she doubtlessly intended to cheer me up. "You are the best kitty in the world, yes you are," I gushed. Then I remembered the woman with the Angora in a carrier. *Of course I'll never be that bad!*

I took another brownie from the box and left Cleo to her play. Curled up in my favorite chair, I turned on the TV. Nothing could soothe the mind and make life seem right like *The Andy Griffith Show.*

"That house is haunted! There are noises and footsteps and the eyes in the picture follow you around..."

I pushed the off button in exasperation. *Of course, it would have to be that episode. Are my thoughts influencing the airwaves or what?* I wasn't going to try another channel, because I just knew a documentary about witch-hunting would be on. Instead, I called Katy. "This is all your fault!" I said when she picked up the phone.

"It usually is. What are you talking about this time?"

"You took me to that fair, introduced me to Cal and then told me all about my dream! Now it's happening again. I saw a portrait today at the gallery. I touched it, and I-I imagined things."

"Imagined or *felt*?"

"What difference does it make? It was very unpleasant. And I can't stop thinking about it now."

"Maybe that's because you're trying too hard. As long as you keep fighting this, you're going to be torn in two. Now listen, Lily. You know I love you and only want you to be happy. You've gone the route with therapy and pills and denial. Is that working? I don't think so."

"Well, I—"

"You connected with Cal, and you had the wolf dream. Now you're having visions again. It's not your imagination, and you know it. I believe you're a true psychic. What if you worked with others who could help you get it under control? Wouldn't it be easier than this limbo you've been in?"

Part of me knew she was right, but part of me was still scared. *What will my mother think? What will Dr. Carson and Stephen say?*

As if she were the psychic reading my mind, Katy spoke again. "You can't live your life doing what others want. I know Stephen and the doctors all have your best interests at heart, but it's time you listen to *your* heart. Why don't you call Cal tomorrow and tell him what happened and why it scared you? He may be able to help."

"I guess." Cal *had* made a favorable impression on me. He was intelligent, grounded and a sympathetic listener. It wouldn't hurt to talk to him again. "Okay, I will. Maybe I'll invite him over. You can be here too."

"Now why would you need me? Are you trying to protect your virtue or matchmaking?"

"I don't want him to get the wrong idea. Anyway, he's gorgeous and nice and a physicist! You gave your approval after I told you all about him. He could help you decide about McKenzie."

Katy laughed. "By telling my future or sweeping me into his manly arms?"

"Who knows? You'll just have to find out. What night is good for you?"

"I don't remember agreeing, but all right. I'm free on Thursday and Friday. Just fill me in after you make the plans."

"Thanks." I heard loud noises from the kitchen. "I've got to go now. Cleo's into something. Bye."

I went to investigate and found my pet up on the counter, trying to drink the glass of milk I'd forgotten. A trail of destruction lay in her wake. The box of brownies was on the floor, two pots had rolled into the sink, and a banana lying beside her was full of bite marks. She had knocked over the flour canister, so it looked like Christmas in October. A white coating covered everything, including the fur of my jet-black cat.

I stared at her for a moment in shock. She ignored me, still trying to fit her head in the glass. I drew in my breath. "Cleocatra Evans! What in the world do you think you're doing?" I picked her up, and she protested vigorously, shaking and squirming until I, too, was decorated with flour dust. "Bad girl! You're going to get a bath for this."

My hyperactive pet suddenly went completely limp in my arms and started trying to lick my face.

"Oh no," I said. "You think it's that easy? What a mess! How much catnip did you get anyway?" A quick glance around me answered that question. The mouse lay in tatters on the floor, with nothing recognizable left except for one pathetic ear. "Oh, Cleo! Did you *have* to do that? Haven't you ever heard of moderation?"

She gazed up at me. *Excuse me, but aren't you the one who ate six chocolate chip cookies in a row yesterday?*

"Well, what if I did?" I replied to the unspoken accusation. "I needed a little pick-me-up. Besides, no one had to pick up after me!"

I put her into the washroom while I cleaned the kitchen and brushed myself off. "Your turn!" I called to Cleo, fetching her grooming kit. I opened the door and found her curled up in the clothes basket, right on top of a fresh load of laundry. *How could I have forgotten that was sitting there?*

My blood pressure shot up before I heard her purring, her eyes blinking in sleepy innocence and her tongue lolling halfway out of her mouth. She looked so adorable I couldn't even yell at her. "All right," I said, giving in. "Go ahead and sleep it off. But you *will* be cleaned before dinner."

As I closed the door and turned away, I could've sworn I heard a faint snort of feline laughter.

Chapter Five

I felt a little sad as I began preparations for dinner the next night. The last meal I'd cooked for a man had been for Kent. That was three months earlier, although it seemed like a lifetime ago. God, how I missed him! He'd been so understanding, so patient with the bizarre circumstances. I could clearly remember every word he had said before taking the plane home to England.

"I don't want to put any pressure on you, Lily. I know you have a lot to sort out. You've got to take care of your mother first and then work out what you want to do. I can't make that decision for you, and neither can Stephen. You need time and space."

He'd had to pause before he continued. "It's okay. It's not going to make me stop loving you. I'll be here if you need me, and I'm not going to be so noble as to insist on silence between us. I've got to stay in touch with you and know that you're all right. Will email be suitable? We can write to each other, can't we?"

I'd nodded, the lump in my throat too big to speak.

"Right then," he'd said softly. "You'll hear from me. Goodbye for now."

Tears had flowed down my face as I'd hugged him tightly. He'd kissed the salt from my lips.

"You'll be brilliant, Lily Evans, I know it."

"I love you, Kent." I had tried trying hopelessly to control myself so he wouldn't remember me as a quivering wreck, but my heart was being pulled and stretched like a piece of taffy. I was lucky to still be standing after all that had happened to me.

"And I love you. Cheers." A final squeeze, a sad smile, and he was gone.

I pushed the memory out of my mind and began pounding steaks with perhaps too much force. Cleocatra stood by, hoping for a tidbit to fall her way. She upped the ante by rubbing against my leg and purring.

"You're not getting any steak," I informed her. "When I'm finished, you can have your own dinner—delicious, nutritious, gourmet cat food!"

Cleo turned up her nose and went under the kitchen table to watch me.

I worked until a palatable meal had taken shape. After putting it on to cook, I kept my promise and opened up a can of Fancy Fixins. Cleo observed me with the air of one who was about to be poisoned. Once it was in her dish, she sniffed at it and turned away.

"Fine. You'll eat when you get hungry enough."

I went upstairs to check my email. Every time I turned on my computer, I felt a tug at my heart. *Has he written?* I scrolled through the messages until his name leapt out at me. *He has!* My fingers trembled a little as I clicked on it. Katy had me foolishly afraid to see an announcement of his forthcoming marriage, but no. His tone was the same as always, affectionate without any pressure. I read his words hungrily:

Dear Lily, I hope you are well. Have you been doing any painting or drawing? Everyone who sees your pictures here loves them. I have your sketch in my office, the one you did of Sunny Hill Gardens. Whenever I look at it I remember that wonderful day. I hope you don't mind, but I passed your name and address along to a few people who have admired Gram's pictures. It's a good time for some commissions before you go back to school. Hope it's not too cheeky of me.

Have you read about the new tomb discovered in Veii? I'm going to be examining some of those pieces soon. I'm over the moon about it. I'll send you the reports, as I know how anxious you are to learn all you can about the Etruscans.

Gram is in Greenland. She took it into her head to go see icebergs and glacial fields. I can't imagine why, but if it makes her happy, that's fine. Winston has been left in charge of Phil and me, because there is no telling what mischief we might get into.

Must run now, I have an appointment at five with one of the museum directors. Write me soon and let me know what you're up to. Love, Kent.

I cried a little, the way I did at every letter. Missing him was an ache that never disappeared. I knew he was worried about my monetary situation and was sending patrons my way in the hope of giving me some support. I smiled at the thought of the intrepid Dame Ursula trekking off to Greenland at the age of eighty-four. She was the most formidable woman I'd ever met, even if I had thought she was crazy at first.

Winston was the family's gourmet cook and general factotum. It was comical to think of that lugubrious man "in charge" of the respectable Phil and easygoing Kent. With no family to speak of except my mother and two aunts I hardly ever saw, it had been fun to spend time with Kent's kinfolk.

I read the letter again and sighed. The doorbell rang downstairs. I hurried to find Katy balancing a tray in one hand.

"Here's your dessert, specially made for the occasion."

I took the tray and peeked under the foil. "Cupcakes."

"Not just cupcakes. Funcakes! See? They're all different colors, and they have sprinkles."

"They're beautiful. And so, might I add, are you."

Katy was wearing a short black skirt and a russet cashmere sweater. She did indeed look spectacular with her long legs and slim figure, her sleek blonde hair brushed back to show a pair of autumn leaf earrings.

"All of this just to impress me?"

"Ha-ha." Katy came in and deposited the cupcakes on the kitchen table. "Mm. What are you cooking? Smells glorious."

"Smothered steak, potatoes au gratin and green beans. I'll make the salad last."

"Good. Don't forget to change!"

"Why? What's wrong with this?" I gestured at my new jeans and navy cardigan.

"Oh, nothing, if you're planning to clean out your closets. But don't forget, we have a gentleman caller coming."

"I'm sorry, Scarlett. I didn't realize we were having a ball at Tara. Let me go pull down the curtains in the living room."

"Do you need help?" Katy asked.

"No. Just sit and try to stay out of trouble."

I took rolls from the freezer to begin thawing.

Katy picked up a cupcake and licked off the icing.

"Can't you wait until after dinner?" I scolded.

"I'm hungry. I had a very early lunch today." She held the plate out to me. "You want one?"

"Of course." I picked one with green streaks and pink frosting and bit into it. "Yummy. Get some milk."

Katy poured two glasses, and we both ate another cupcake.

"Now that's positively it." I put the plate on top of the refrigerator. "We're not going to spoil our appetites after all of this work."

"Your mascara is smudged," Katy scrutinized, "and your nose is red. What happened?"

I sighed. "Kent wrote. You know how his letters always make me feel."

Katy was sympathetic. "I do. Anything out of the ordinary?"

"Not really, unless you count his grandmother going off to Greenland."

"For that family, that *is* ordinary. I'm sorry."

No more words were needed between us. I went to freshen up my makeup. When I got back to the kitchen, Katy had half a cupcake in her mouth and was feeding Cleocatra crumbs.

"Honestly! I can't take my eyes off you two for a minute."

"It was Cleo," Katy mumbled. "She made me."

"Go in the living room, both of you."

"You heard her, Cleo. Shoo."

I looked at Katy sternly. "If you're going to stay in here, you have to work. Please set the table. We're using real napkins for our gentleman caller."

"Right-o. What about wine? I didn't notice any in the refrigerator."

"Cal is bringing the wine. I told him you drink like a fish."

"Lily Ann Evans, you did not!"

I laughed. "No, but I will if you touch one more cupcake."

By the time Cal arrived, we had everything ready. I took him on a tour of the house, and he admired the many pictures I had on the walls. Some were paintings I'd done myself, but most were prints with Egyptian themes. He was duly impressed by the dinner and by Katy. She had reinterpreted the cards in the druid's tent to mean she should take a chance on Caliman. Poor McKenzie was now completely out of the equation.

I couldn't blame her. Cal was a fascinating man. He talked about his work in a way that we could understand, without ever sounding condescending.

"Some scientists think there could be an infinite number of parallel universes," he said as we sipped our wine, "worlds exactly like Earth, with copies of all of us walking around on them. They might be living the same lives or lives just slightly different. Maybe you take a right turn instead of a left. Or lives very different, where you join a rock band and become a superstar instead of going to college."

"I remember Bono saying once to Charlie Rose that if he weren't a musician, he would probably be living under a bridge somewhere." Katy was a huge fan of U2. "Charlie Rose scoffed at the idea."

Cal smiled at her. "In an infinite universe, every possibility plays out. Somewhere right now, I could be sitting down to dinner with the two of you, but we'd be eating fish instead of this wonderful steak, drinking green wine and feeding your dog tidbits under the table."

There was a sudden loud *meow*. I laughed. "Cleo doesn't like that idea at all."

"Well, I've seen it on *Doctor Who*," Katy observed. "I can believe it."

"I love *Doctor Who*!" Cal said. Katy grinned. It was romance blooming right before my eyes.

Cal was a good listener too, and took time to ask Katy questions about her work. "I've attended a few of the lectures given by Dr. White. What a brilliant man."

"Oh, he is," Katy agreed reverently. "The perfect person to head up the Arthur project. He's the world's leading authority. What I wouldn't give to be his assistant!"

"Well, in another reality, maybe you are," I remarked, "and the She-Beast works for *you*!"

"That's what I call my boss, Dr. Webster," Katy confided to Cal. "But never mind her. I don't want to spoil my appetite. So…you're interested in the Arthurian cycle too?"

"My mom read the stories to me when I was a kid, in all their forms. She's very proud of her Welsh heritage, so we both know the *Mabinogian* by heart."

"The what?"

Katy turned a pitying look upon me, and Cal laughed. "Your last name is Evans, and you don't recognize Wales's greatest literary treasure? For shame!"

Katy addressed me with an exaggerated sigh. "Allow me to enlighten you, poor girl. The *Mabinogian* is a collection of stories from the medieval period, based on older Welsh folklore and legend. The tales contain the earliest forms of Arthur. They're an invaluable source of information about Celtic history and mythology."

"Thank you, Professor Morrison. I can see you and Dr. Jones will have plenty to discuss."

"So you really are like a druid, Cal," Katy said. "You can recite ancient lore, you study cosmology and you possess great knowledge."

"And a white robe. Don't forget that!"

He was charming. The only female impervious to him was Cleocatra, who had hidden behind the sofa as soon as he appeared. Not even some leftover steak on a plate could coax her out again. "Sorry." I shrugged. "She's pretty much a one-man cat, and that man is Stephen."

"It's all right." Cal smiled. "I won't take it personally."

The conversation then turned inevitably to the strange portrait in the gallery. I told him how much it had frightened me, how I had seen the eyes again in my car mirror and how the wolf had appeared on the sidewalk. Katy explained how we had nearly run over one in the road. "And then I saw him again in a dream," I said. "Wolves everywhere!"

"They're a symbol of something, aren't they?" Katy asked. "I told her it was a transformation dream."

"It certainly sounds like it," Cal agreed. "For better or worse, Lily, meeting me opened a gate for you. I don't think you could shut it again without doing irreparable harm to your psyche. You're meant to take this journey, and I'll help you in any way I can."

"Well, how about coming over to the gallery with me? Then we can look at the picture together." I glanced at Katy. "Is that all right with you?"

"Sure, but I'll skip the art, if you don't mind. I need to do some shopping at the store next door. Somebody's birthday is getting close!"

"I knew it," Cal said to me. "You have Libra written all over you."

"What? An astrophysicist who believes in star signs?" I teased. "That must be part of the druid legacy."

"Indeed. I have to cover all the bases. Let me help you clean up."

"No, no," I protested as I rose from the table. "You're a guest. Stay and talk to Katy."

"I insist." Cal stood and started gathering dishes. "You've already worked hard making this wonderful meal. It's the least I can do."

"He's right, Lily. You sit and relax. I know where everything goes."

I hid my smile as they disappeared into the kitchen. Katy seldom offered her

assistance. Although she was a meticulous scholar, she was not the neatest person in the world. But I suspected she would have scrubbed the floor with a toothbrush if Cal were beside her.

"Thank you," I said when they were finished. "Did you see the cupcakes Katy brought, Cal? We could take them with us if you'd like."

"We already ate them," Katy replied. "I knew you wouldn't want any more after all you had before dinner."

I let the shameless remark go. "Whose car are we taking?"

Katy volunteered to drive, and I got in the back seat before Cal had a choice in the matter. The two of them discussed the transmigration of souls while I stared out the window, absorbed in my own thoughts. They both had important academic careers to focus on and enjoy. It made me realize how much I missed my Egyptian studies and the stimulation of university life.

Maybe I should audit one or two classes just to get back into the swing of things. But then, what kind of reception would I get? Would people point and whisper? After all, I was the one who'd exposed Professor Briggs as an antiquities thief. A famous and profit-producing member of the faculty was gone after a very public brawl with my boyfriend. It was my mother who'd taken the artifacts and given them to Briggs in the first place. *No. I'm not quite ready for school again yet.*

When we arrived at the gallery, Katy practically skipped off to the craft store, but I was filled with foreboding. I found I was afraid to carry out my mission. I remembered the screaming, the fire and the sense of evil.

Cal saw my hesitation and understood. "I can go in alone if you'd like. Would you rather be with Katy?"

I thought for a moment and then shook my head. "No. I brought you here, and I'm not running away."

"Good. Come on then."

No one else was in the gallery. As we walked towards the portrait, Cal caught sight of my picture of Thoth. "Now that definitely looks Egyptian. It's yours, isn't it?"

"Yes." I was pleased that he'd noticed it. "He's the god of wisdom and writing."

"It's beautiful." He admired it for a minute. "Are there any more?"

I showed him the other one, and he asked me about its subject matter. I was grateful for the attempt to put me more at ease. But at last I had to guide him to the portrait.

Cal looked at it for a long time, and I looked at Cal. I didn't want to see the eyes in the picture again. His face was inscrutable as he touched it. *Why doesn't he seem to be affected?*

Then, all of a sudden, his expression softened. He glanced at me with a sad little smile. "I think I understand your feelings. What came through to you was one of the most horrific things a person could endure. The psychic residue of such an event is enormous. No wonder it scared you so much."

"It's not my imagination then?" I didn't know whether to be relieved or disappointed. "Is she evil?"

Cal shook his head. "There's evil all right, but I'd say this woman was the *victim* of it, not the source. If it's really from the seventeenth century, it could have been painted about the time of the witch hunts. You picked up on shouting and chanting and fear, right? Then heat and flames? It could have been the echo of a crowd dragging their human sacrifice to the stake. They must have burned her as a witch."

I shuddered. "How could anyone do that? Stand there and watch while…ugh!" I forced the image from my mind. "I knew something terrible had happened, but I guess I didn't want to believe it."

"I don't blame you. I don't want to put any pressure on you here, but it seems this lady still has something important to say. She's obviously not at rest. Would you be willing to help her?"

I shrank away from the thought. She was not Amisihathor, the young Egyptian woman I'd felt such empathy for. I didn't know the person in the portrait, and what I'd sensed didn't make me want to. *Still, if Cal's right and she's was a lost soul who needs to find peace...* "I've got to be honest with you," I said. "The emotions were so strong, so powerful. I'm not sure I can handle it."

"Fair enough. It's up to you what you feel comfortable with. I can ask the other people in my group, as long as the owner doesn't mind us coming in here."

"Carolyn's a sweetheart. I'll tell her I have friends who want to study the portrait. I'd like to help. I just—"

"Don't give it another thought. You're new at this. You can't be expected to take on such a challenge. But if you want to learn, I'd welcome your being here as an observer."

"I guess I'd like to be here. It will be interesting to see what someone else picks up on and how they handle it."

"Okay. I'll tell you what. We'll meet over at my house beforehand, and you can see who you'll be working with. They're nice people, and I'm sure you'll like them. Just let me coordinate it, and I'll set a time with you. How's that?"

"Fine. Now we'd better go and get Katy."

I couldn't help but be relieved on the drive home. I hadn't expected Cal to take on the burden of the painting by himself, but I was selfishly glad he had. Frankly, it terrified me. It was strange how our feelings about the woman varied. I saw evil *in* her, while Cal saw it *around* her. He was much more experienced than I was, and he was probably right, but I was still happy I wouldn't have to face those eyes again.

He stayed for a few minutes after we got back to the house. Cleocatra, who had ventured forth and eaten all of the steak, jumped off my armchair and went behind the sofa. I shook my head and picked up the dirty plate. I took a long time cleaning it in the kitchen so Katy and Cal could have a few more minutes alone.

When I came out, they were smiling at each other, and Katy's face was glowing. *He's asked her on a date*, I thought.

Sure enough, once he'd left after profuse thanks for the dinner, Katy turned to me in excitement. "We're going to the movies Saturday night! Oh, Lily, isn't he wonderful? He knows so much about everything! He's the smartest man I've ever met—not to mention the best looking."

"And he's nice," I added. "I really like him. As long as you don't mind having your thoughts read, you should be fine."

"He doesn't do that without permission. If he did, he'd have been blushing from head to toe. Thanks for inviting me tonight. It was great."

"Thanks for coming. No one felt awkward this way. I can return the favor at the movies if you want me to."

"Lily Evans, you keep your hands off my man, or I might have to tear out all that gorgeous brown hair. Love you!" She blew me a kiss. "Goodnight."

I went upstairs after she'd gone, Cleocatra trailing after me. I sat down at the computer to answer Kent's letter with the words "my man" echoing in my head. *If only I could see my man again, feel his arms around me, and...*

But there was no use thinking that way. *If wishes were horses, then beggars could ride.* My horse would have been galloping faster than Seabiscuit. I typed in my reply:

Dear Kent, I'm glad you'll soon have more Etruscans to play with. I know how exciting that is for you. I wish I could say I have some ancient Egyptians coming to visit, but that door is shut to me right now. However, I have found an most interesting portrait...

Chapter Six

Cal hosted a get-together on Friday night the following week. We gathered at his house so I could meet some of the people involved in his group. They each had their own unique background and story.

Derek Thayer was an Englishman who worked as an actor in the city theater company. I guessed his age to be about thirty, but his hair was already completely white. He wore it in a brush cut and sported a gold hoop through one ear. "This is as strange a maze as e'er men trod," he greeted me.

A tall, thin girl rebuked him. "She's brand new, for pity's sake. Don't start quoting Shakespeare at her first thing!"

Derek grinned. "Sorry, love. Learning my lines for *The Tempest*. I'm playing Antonio. And this fair maiden..." He swept a bow at the thin girl. "...is Mistress Amelia Scott, purveyor of fine comestibles."

"He means I'm in the restaurant business. And it's Amy."

"Hi, Amy. I'm Lily Evans."

"So I guessed. I am psychic, after all." She indicated a stunning blonde sitting on the sofa beside her. "Yvette Alexander. She works in physics with Cal."

Even at such a casual meeting, Yvette was dressed in a tailored two-piece outfit with perfect makeup and a jade necklace that matched the color of her eyes. She gave me a searching glance and then seemed to dismiss me.

"I'm Jo Levinson." A petite woman with close-cropped curly hair and a friendly smile shook my hand. "We left our robes and pointed hats at home tonight so as not to scare you, but if you measure up, you'll get your very own. Only one color available, I'm afraid—basic black. Yvette wouldn't stand for anything else because it sets off her hair and skin so well."

"I hear you already have a black cat," Amy said. "That only leaves a crystal ball and a magic wand."

"And wouldn't you know it, Witches"R"Us is having a sale this week," Jo added.

"Cal says you have quite a gift, Lily. Can you tell us about it?" Derek asked.

Jo rapped on the side of her wineglass with the fork from the cheese tray. "Attention! Attention please! Lily Evans has the floor! Or the sofa, to be more exact."

Everyone stopped talking and turned their heads toward me. It felt a little awkward to be the center of attention, but after all, it was what I was there for.

"Well," I began, "ever since I was a little girl, I've felt a strong kinship for ancient Egypt. When I heard or read about it, it felt like I was there. I drew pictures of houses and statues and people. Sometimes I dreamt of playing by the side of the Nile, learning to draw hieroglyphs, or talking to people who seemed like my family." I paused and took a sip of my wine.

"It wasn't until a few months ago, when a famous archaeologist came to the city, that I found out I was creating sketches and paintings of real places. She—Dame Ursula Allingham—recognized scenes from a tomb she'd excavated. Somehow I had tuned into the life of a woman who lived over three and a half thousand years ago. Her name was Amisihathor, and her relics were being displayed at the museum. Dame Ursula arranged for me to have a private viewing, and I picked up a necklace and…well, I started to see through Amisihathor's eyes."

For a moment, my mind drifted back to that intense experience. I had to shake myself mentally before I could continue.

"The last months of her life played out before me in dreams and visions. I discovered what had happened to her and why she wasn't at peace. I was able to help her, and that was a wonderful feeling, but the process wasn't easy. In the end, it was horrible. I was physically ill and almost died. It scared me so much that I decided it would be better to forget the whole thing. I wanted to be cured. I wanted to be…normal."

Jo spoke up first. "I don't think there's one of us who hasn't felt that way, especially when you're a kid and desperate to fit in. My mom was a psychic too, but she was so frightened by her gifts that she repressed them in herself and in me. She didn't want to discuss it. She didn't want to help me understand. 'Fight it,' she told me. 'Ignore it.'"

"That was my first reaction too," I said.

Jo nodded. "But it turned out to be so much harder than just giving in. I couldn't ignore it, and it exhausted me to try. I ended up doing my own research as a teenager and never mentioned it to Mom. When I went to college, I got involved in psychic research and experimentation. For the first time, I was welcomed for who I was, and now this group has accepted me." She smiled around at everyone. "I never feel alone anymore."

"Me neither," Amy said. "I learned very early not to talk about my invisible friends to anyone. Now people actually want to know!"

"I was lucky," Yvette informed me in a clear, cool voice. "My parents recognized my talents and had me tested. I grew up among paranormal researchers. It was no different from a regular doctor visit or my ballet lessons—simply something I did, part of my ordinary life. I even told my friends' fortunes. They loved it. I've never felt like an outcast."

Well, why would she? Beautiful, smart, and surrounded by people who understood and supported her. She has been lucky. I reminded myself that it was wrong to judge, but I couldn't help feeling a slight dislike for Yvette. *Do I sense some animosity in her? Is that why?*

Derek and Amy, as I came to find out, were mediums. They attended a Spiritualist church and presided over séances.

"Isn't it frightening to feel someone else taking control of you?" I asked.

"Oh, they don't take control, love," Derek replied. "We let them in, and they speak *through* us, but our own consciousness is always there. And just in case, there are spirit guides who protect us. I've never been possessed. Maybe threatened on rare occasions, but then I just shut them out. It's like opening and closing a mental door."

"You have to practice though," Amy explained. "I was so green at first that I had some trouble. But the other members helped me out, and I grew strong enough to believe in myself. Now I just love helping or comforting others. I wouldn't trade that gift for anything."

There were nods of agreement all around. I felt a cold place inside of me begin to thaw out. *What if it's a gift and not a form of insanity to be wiped away with pills and therapy?* I wasn't sure yet, but I definitely liked the idea.

We talked for a while longer, comparing notes, and then it was time to go. We piled into two different cars, Cal driving one and Jo the other. I was in the back seat of hers, with Derek beside me for company. We kept up a lively conversation and speculated about what might happen. It felt rather like going on a field trip for school.

"My dad loved Shakespeare," I told Derek. "I still have his old college textbooks with his notes in the margins. I started reading them when I was twelve. I memorized some of Juliet's lines and pretended that the front porch was a balcony."

"And who was your Romeo?" Derek asked with a smile.

"The boy who lived next door. He played along, even though he thought I was crazy."

"Ah, young love."

"He was in love all right…with my mom's baking!"

When we reached the gallery, I greeted Carolyn and introduced everyone. "I'll just be doing some inventory in the back," she said. "Let me know if you need me."

"Thanks, Carolyn. And thanks again for letting us in after closing."

The first thing everyone did was look at my paintings. Cal must have told them they were here, and I couldn't help but be pleased at their words of admiration. Yvette, however, barely glanced at them. She made straight for the portrait, and eventually the others joined her.

"First," Caliman said, "we call down the white light of protection. Join hands."

He took one of my hands and one of Yvette's. Everyone bowed their heads.

"We ask for all the good spirits to protect us and keep us from harm. Surround us with light and love and keep any who would wish to harm us at bay. Bless us all. Thank you."

He lifted his head and looked at me. "This is very important, Lily. You're opening yourself to powerful forces, and you can't risk letting them take over. Visualize the white light going through you and making you safe. Wrap it around yourself. Can you do it? Can you feel its presence?"

I could indeed. It wasn't difficult for me because of my yoga and meditation practices. "Yes, I can feel it."

"Good. Then we can begin. Who'd like to go first?"

"I will." Jo stood and gazed at the portrait. "I come with respect and the desire to help." She then reached out and touched it lightly.

It wasn't long before a spasm of pain crossed her face, and she pulled her hand away quickly. "Oh my God! How horrible! They burned the house with her in it. She was shouting, screaming, but the crowd was so loud, and no one listened. Wait…" Jo leaned againt the wall for support. "Just give me a minute." She took some deep breaths while the others patted her shoulders reassuringly. Then she closed her eyes and stood perfectly still.

"She's centering herself," Cal whispered to me. "It's possible to distance yourself from the emotions that way."

Soon, Jo was ready to go on. I watched in admiration as she touched the portrait again.

"She was a healer," Jo continued in a much calmer tone. "She loved animals. She took care of anything hurt or frightened. She had a way with them, and they came onto her land. She had a big house outside of town on the edge of the woods. She lived there with a man, her husband Thomas. She looked after him too. He wasn't strong—something with the lungs. It seems they were quite well off."

"Can she tell you her name?" Cal asked. "Or what year it is?"

"No." Jo shook her head. "I'm not getting that. The smoke and the fire are coming back." She gave a shudder and drew her hand away.

"It's all right," Cal said. "You don't have to go on. We've learned a lot already. Don't force yourself."

Jo looked at me apologetically. "Sorry, but an important lesson is knowing when to stop."

"You've been amazing, Jo. And now you'll just be able to let it go?" I couldn't imagine how everything she'd seen wouldn't haunt her.

"Yes. Oh, I'll be tired, but I've learned to separate myself from my subjects. It just takes practice and the protection of the light."

"It's really not so different from your doctor friend Stephen or any other person who deals with trauma in their jobs," Cal said. "You have to have strong defenses or you couldn't do it anymore."

That made sense to me. I knew Stephen still struggled sometimes, especially when children were involved, but he'd found a way to cope with it, to protect himself and still care. I wished I could talk to him about all of what I was learning, but I knew that was out of the question.

"Derek, do you want to try?" Cal asked.

Derek approached the portrait the way a wrestler steps into the ring. He did not touch it but stared fixedly at the beautiful face. Then he closed his eyes, and—in a minute—began to speak. "She had a wolf."

I gasped, but no one seemed to notice.

Derek's voice went on. "He was lame when she found him as a pup. She cured his leg and raised him. He was devoted to her, followed her wherever she went—a great, gray beast. He made Thomas nervous, but she loved the animal dearly."

"Are there any clues as to her identity?" Jo asked.

"No."

"Let me try," I said, inspired by the others.

"Are you sure, Lily?" Cal asked.

"Yes. I have all of you with me, and I'll stop if it gets too intense."

"All right. But give me your hand first."

I did so, and Cal held it while he looked into my eyes. Apparently satisfied, he said, "Now remember, the light is all around you. Feel it. You are protected."

I nodded and drew in a deep breath before I reached out.

This time, I did not sense overwhelming violence and hatred. I saw the same woman, but she was wearing a yellow dress, and her glorious hair was hidden under a white bonnet. She was stirring a large iron pot over a fireplace, putting in the various ingredients for stew. A wolf was standing by, just as Cleocatra did when I cooked. Every now and then, the woman dropped a small bit of meat, and the animal gulped it down.

I smiled as I thought of my own pet. The scene I was seeing in the kitchen was a happy one, totally unlike my last experience with the painting. The woman was humming as she worked, as if she was glad to be creating something for the man she loved. Suddenly, she turned her head, and those great brown eyes looked right into mine. I felt a shock of familiarity.

"I am called Rose," she said, "Mistress Rose Woodbine. But he is coming now, and I can show you no more."

I started and felt Cal's arm come around my shoulders. "Lily, are you all right?"

I turned my gaze on him and was back in the art gallery, with everyone staring at me. "I'm fine. I was just watching her make dinner. Her name is Rose Woodbine."

"That's wonderful!" Cal exclaimed. "She let you in so quickly. Traumatic emotions are relatively easy to read, but everyday scenes are more difficult. She must trust you. Didn't I say from the beginning that you have a good soul?"

I looked away modestly and caught Yvette frowning. *Aha!* I didn't have to be psychic to know what was going on there.

My eyes went back to Cal. "She knew I was watching her too. She told me her name and then asked me to leave. Her husband was coming, and she wanted to be alone with him."

"We all saw you smile," Amy said. "Rose must have felt very happy."

"I think she did, but I was smiling because of the wolf. He was getting tidbits from the pot, just like my cat does."

"You saw the wolf too?" Derek was excited. "It's great when we can back each other up."

"And I can do research now," Jo said. "We'll see what the records have to tell us." She loved digging into history and gathering facts.

"Okay," Cal announced, "I think we can call it a night. We did some excellent work. When we know more about Rose, we can figure out how to help her. You were fantastic, Lily, facing your fear like that. You already seem more comfortable."

"I am, thanks to all of you. I'm so glad we met."

"We'll get together again soon," Cal promised.

Yvette stepped over and put her arm through his. "Who's riding with us?" she asked.

Amy followed them out the door.

I went to say goodbye to Carolyn and then set off with Derek and Jo. We chatted until we reached Cal's house, where we all went our separate ways.

The others had advised me to close my mind for the rest of the night and relax. I put in a CD and sang along as I drove home. When Rose's face appeared before me, I practiced shutting my mental door. It worked for the most part, but I couldn't help comparing how different my two experiences with her had been.

I supposed Cal was right. I'd felt the fear and hatred of the mob the first time, but Rose had certainly not been threatening on my second attempt. Even her very features seemed to have changed, softening and leaving only beauty there. I didn't want to think about her final days. *Slam the door on that. Lock it and throw away the key.* Only when it was time and I had the protection of the group would I open myself to her again.

Chapter Seven

"A Halloween party?" I asked in surprise. Stephen and I were sitting in the little inn on campus, the one I'd introduced him to, eating Greek food. I looked at him through narrowed eyes. "I could never get you to dress up for a party. You said it was silly. The only thing you ever liked about Halloween was carving the pumpkins. You said it was good practice."

"I know," he admitted. "I was a bit of a stick-in-the-mud, but this is different. It's for the children. It was Jenny's idea. The staff is going to hand out treats, and then we'll have our own party in the conference room. It'll be fun. You can wear your Cleopatra outfit if you still have it."

"Oh I still have it, but what are you going to be?"

"What else? A knight in shining armor, and Jenny is a damsel in distress."

"Isn't that cute?" *Damsel in distress indeed.* She could probably slay a few dragons without getting a hair out of place.

"Katy can come as Guinevere," Stephen went on. "Jenny's sister is going to be a black cat. Her costume is adorable."

My fork stopped halfway to my lips. Stephen had never used words like "adorable." *Jenny should appear as the cat,* I thought. *She certainly has her claws dug firmly into him.*

"Well, that sounds like fun. I'll keep it in mind. Thanks for asking."

"Find the book," Stephen said irrelevantly.

"Which book?" *Is there some kind of instruction manual I've forgotten about?* Costume Parties for Dummies *or something?*

"Which book what?" He looked confused.

"You just told me to find the book. What book are you talking about?"

He shook his head. "Honey, maybe it's time for you to cut back on your meds. I didn't say anything about a book. We were talking about the Halloween party, remember?"

"Stephen Mallory, I know what I heard. You must have been thinking out loud without realizing it."

"Um…I guess so," he agreed in an utterly unconvincing tone, "but on a completely different subject, when *was* the last time you saw Dr. Carson?"

"A couple weeks ago, and he thought everything was going well. I hope you're not implying that I'm imagining or hearing things."

"No, no. Sorry. Forget it." He checked his watch and gulped down the last of his drink. "I've got to be getting back. Thanks for meeting me. This place is a real treat. I'll pay the bill on the way out."

"Hold on. I'll have them wrap the rest of mine to go so I can walk back with you." I motioned to our waitress, who quickly supplied me with a plastic container. "Now I won't have to cook any dinner."

It was a beautiful day in the most beautiful season of the year; Autumn had always been my favorite. The university campus was filled with old trees that turned every color, and I could hardly look at them enough. I had to drink in the red and orange and gold before November came creeping and stripped the branches bare.

The leaves that had already wafted to the ground crunched under our feet. The sky was a rich blue, no longer bleached by summer's heat. The ivy-covered brick buildings and the bronze statues in front of them lent the impression of strolling through a nineteenth-century landscape. It really was one of the country's most gorgeous college campuses. The whole world seemed golden.

Stephen took my hand, and I felt a sudden rush of affection for him. I hoped Jenny would turn out to be good enough for my dear friend. We parted at my car, and Stephen continued the short walk from campus to the hospital.

Just as I was about to turn the key in the ignition, my cell phone rang. "Hi," said Katy. "Want to go to lunch? The She-Beast is off today, so I can take as long as I want."

"Sorry, but I just finished lunch with Stephen. How about a walk along the river?"

"Um, no. I want to eat a nice leisurely meal and relax. Hey, I think I'll ask Cal. Do you happen to have his cell number handy?"

"Aha! So that's your ulterior motive. Hang on. I'll see where I wrote it down." I rummaged in my purse for my address book. "Just what would you have done if I'd have accepted your invitation?"

"Oh, I'd have suffered through it, thinking of Cal all the time!"

"Very nice. He's at 747-8849. You two seem to have really hit it off. I see McKenzie becoming a distant memory."

"Well come on, Lily. Cal is pretty fantastic, isn't he? He promised to call, but I don't feel like waiting. What if I got hit by a bus tomorrow and missed my chance at true love?"

I laughed. "You certainly have a unique outlook on life. I hope he's free and that you have a wonderful lunch."

"Thanks. Oh, and don't forget to find the book."

She clicked off, leaving me standing and staring at mine in awe. *Another cryptic reference to a book?* I called her back quickly, but the line was already busy.

Now don't get excited. She meant a real book, one we must have already talked about. I searched my memory for anything I might have borrowed from her or anything of mine that she could want. I came up empty on both counts. I decided I'd try her again later. *No problem*, I tried to tell myself, but as I started the car and drove home, a nagging uneasiness lingered in the back of my mind.

My next-door neighbor Christine was out raking leaves when I got to the house. She gave a friendly wave, and her two dogs, a cockapoo and a terripoo, rushed at me in excitement. "Hello, girls!" I said as they leapt about me with their tails wagging. "How are the little sweeties today?"

"In heaven," Christine replied. "I had to get up to answer the phone and left a piece of pecan pie on the coffee table. I thought I pushed it back far enough, but no. They got to it somehow and ate the whole thing. You think they'd be full after tipping over the trash and gobbling up Kleenex. They'll eat anything but dog food. Won't you, girls?"

Coal-black Spot and tawny Scarlett looked at me with wide, innocent eyes. Their message was as clear as day: *We never do anything wrong.* I petted both of them, and they licked my hands. I could see Cleocatra standing in the window of my house with her back arched, clearly disapproving of my fraternization with the enemy. "I've gotta run, girls, or else Cleo isn't going to speak to me. I'll see you later. Bye, Chris."

"Bye, Lily. I hope you find the book."

I turned back around sharply. "What book?"

But Chris had returned to raking leaves and seemed not to hear me. *This is getting creepier and creepier.*

When I got in my front door, Cleocatra climbed down from the windowsill onto the couch, then jumped to the floor and left the room. I went into the kitchen and got a can of tuna fish. As soon as the electric opener began to hum, Cleo reappeared like a shot. "I thought so," I said as I spooned some into her bowl. "Forgiveness is cheap."

I noticed the red light blinking on the phone and pushed the button to play the messages. The first was a reminder of a doctor's appointment. The second was my friend Moira. "Lily, I wish you'd come back to yoga," she pleaded. "It's so much more fun with you there…and don't forget to find the book."

A little shiver ran through me. *The book again? This is more than coincidence.* I snatched up the phone and tried to call Moira, but she wasn't there. Next I dialed Katy, who answered on the second ring. "Katy," I demanded, "what book were you talking about?"

"Book? What do you mean?" Katy sounded mystified.

"When you called me for Cal's number, the last thing you said before you hung up was 'find the book.' What book?"

"I don't remember saying that. Are you sure?"

"Of course I'm sure! I couldn't figure it out. I didn't borrow anything from you, did I?"

"No, and we weren't talking about any books either. It beats me, Lily."

"Well this is just too weird." I paused. "Did you get a hold of Cal for lunch?"

"No," Katy said, sounding sad. "He's stuck in a meeting, and he's going to the movies with friends tonight. But he promised me tomorrow for sure."

"That's great. I'll talk to you later."

I hung up before she could press me with any questions. Something was going on, of that I was certain. I hesitated a moment, then tried Cal's cell phone. *It can't hurt to leave a message, just to get his opinion.* But to my surprise, he answered himself. "Oh, Cal, I'm sorry," I said. "I didn't mean to interrupt your meeting."

"The meeting's over. We wrapped up early. What's wrong?"

"I don't know. I mean, I'm not certain. Something odd is happening that I don't understand. I was hoping you might have a clue."

"'Odd' as in some kind of psychic experience? You're not being threatened, are you?"

"I don't think so, but it's not like before. It's not me. It's other people. It's really freaking me out."

"Tell you what. I don't have anything on the agenda until tonight. Would you like me to come over?"

"Well…if you're sure you don't mind, I would really appreciate it."

"I'll be there in about half an hour, okay?"

"This is so nice of you. Thanks."

True to his word, he arrived thirty minutes later. "It's good of you to come so quickly," I said as I let him in.

"No problem." He followed me into the living room, and we sat down on the sofa. "You sound a little scared. Tell me what's wrong."

I started with Stephen and then related all of the references to "the book" As Cal listened attentively.

"And you don't have *any* idea what book this is?" he asked.

"None at all, and neither do Stephen or Katy. Chris ignored me. If I called Moira, I'll bet she wouldn't understand either. What do you think is happening?"

"Well, someone's trying to tell you something, and my guess would be it's Rose Woodbine. Who else have you been in psychic contact with?"

"But why wouldn't she just talk to me herself? Or speak through one of the group members?"

"Maybe she knows she frightened you at first and she doesn't want to invade your mind. This is a way to get your attention. If you don't want to contact her directly, we can get everyone together and see who will."

"Okay. That'd be good. I need to find out what's going on."

"I'll call them. But there's no need to worry, Lily. Rose seems to be moving carefully with you. She's planting very brief thoughts in people's brains that they instantly forget. She doesn't want to alarm anyone, especially you."

"That makes me feel better. All of this takes some getting used to, doesn't it?"

"Oh yeah. It's definitely a learning process. I think you're doing remarkably well though."

I smiled at him. "Thanks. You've been a big help to me."

"Glad to be of service." Changing tack, he said, "I'm sorry I didn't get to have lunch with Katy today. How long have you two been friends?"

"It seems like forever, but it's really only been five years. We met at the university when we took a creative writing class together. Katy's very good at it, but let's just say my talents lie in other directions."

"From what I've seen of your work, it's fantastic. Could I look at your Egyptian drawings sometime?"

I still felt some misgivings about all the sketches of Amisihathor's life I'd done in the summer. They brought back Kent too sharply. They also reminded me of what had befallen my mother. I was too ambivalent to share them so soon. "Of course you can, after I dig them up," I hedged.

"Maybe later, when you feel at ease with her, you can capture Rose on paper. You seem to have extra talent as a psychic artist." He must have noticed my tenseness, because he added hurriedly, "Only if you want to, of course. I won't ask you to do anything you're not comfortable with. Everyone's here to help you progress at your own pace."

"I appreciate that. Also, I was wondering, can you recommend some good books for me?"

"Sure. I have a few I can loan you, and I'll make a list of the rest. It's a good idea to gather all the information you can."

"I'm a researcher. I can never have too much information."

"I know that feeling." A strange expression passed across his face, and I had the prickly sense that I'd said something wrong.

I was wondering how to break the awkward silence when Cal spoke again. "Lily, do you ever feel there isn't enough time in the world to learn all that you want to know?"

I considered the question. "Well, before exams and papers are due, I guess. And this paranormal business is pretty overwhelming. But ordinarily, no. I love discovering new stories and facts about Egypt. I enjoy each one as it comes along. There's no pressure to it."

I saw that it wasn't an answer that helped him. He still looked troubled, so I pressed on.

"Of course my field is nowhere near as demanding as yours. It boggles my mind how you keep up. And I'm not a genius either. Your brain must never stop working."

"No. It doesn't. I want—I *need* to understand." His fists clenched unconsciously. "I need to find order in the chaos."

"What's wrong with that? It takes drive to succeed."

"Yes, but..." He trailed off, seemingly on the edge of confiding something to me.

I reached out and touched his arm. "But what?"

A moment passed, and then his features relaxed. "It doesn't matter. Sorry to get off track. I'll call you when I've fixed up a time for a meeting. I'm having dinner with Katy tomorrow, but I'm sure you already know that."

"Guilty." I was a little miffed that he didn't trust me after all the secrets he'd gotten from me. "There's nothing we don't talk about. But don't worry. We won't get *too* personal."

"That's a relief." Cal stood up and held out a hand to me. "I'm sorry, but I've got to be going. I'm meeting a group of friends tonight. Will you be okay?"

"Yes. I feel much better. Thanks again for coming over. I hope you like the movie."

He grinned and shook his head. "Women. I'll talk to you soon."

"Okay." I saw him to the door. The moment it shut behind him, Cleocatra glided into the room. "Oh, so her royal highness has decided to grace us with her presence? What guests can I have that you actually approve of? Never mind. I know the answer to that."

I picked her up and put her over my shoulder like a baby. "Who's a funny little kitty?" I crooned as I stroked her. "It's my little Cleo, queen of all the cats. I love you, yes I do."

She suffered the attention for two minutes before she struggled and I had to set her down. "All right, all right. I'm sorry if I offended your dignity. It could be worse, you know. How would you like it if I put cute costumes on you, then took pictures for magazines? We might be able to win some prizes and go to Kit-N-Kaboodle every week."

I fancied that I heard her in my head. *How would you like it if I ran away from home?*

"No need to start packing," I replied. "I was just kidding. Although, with a golden tiara and collar, you could come to the Halloween party if you promised not to claw Jenny."

Cleo's eyes glittered. Clearly, it was a promise she wouldn't pretend to keep.

Chapter Eight

"And he got a *full* scholarship to the University of Chicago, a perfect score on the SATs, and every science prize in the state. Of course everybody wanted him. But he's not the least bit conceited, is he? He's just so easy to talk to. He knows about history and mythology and all the things I'm interested in. We were on the phone for hours last night. Can you believe it?"

I certainly could. I had been listening to Katy rhapsodize about Cal for our entire lunch. *Was I that bad with Kent? I don't think so.*

"Guess what his favorite color is? Red! Just like mine. Ninety percent of people say their favorite color is blue. I'm glad he's not a blue. I just don't think I could date a blue guy—although he does look good in it, with those amazing eyes. Have you ever seen a more gorgeous man? Of course," she added hastily, "Stephen and Kent are very good looking, but Cal is just…he's so *striking.* I've never met anyone like him. Isn't he great?"

This time she actually paused long enough for me to answer. "He's one of a kind all right. I do like him. His being psychic doesn't bother you at all?"

"He can turn it on and off like a faucet, he says. He'll be able to help you do that too."

"He's been so nice. It's hard to believe you once threatened him with fried dough."

"I was defending *your* honor. I knew he would turn out to be wonderful. He invited me to a Halloween party at the hospital. Seems like most of the university's going to be there. Did Stephen mention it to you?"

"Yes, to tell me he was taking Jenny. Speak of the devil." I nodded toward the other side of the inn. Jenny and Stephen had just come through the door.

Katy gaped, temporarily distracted from her paean to Caliman. "Wow. Isn't she beautiful?"

"She is," I agreed. "I just hope she's nice too."

"Should we go say hello or pretend we don't notice them?"

"Pretend we don't notice. We don't want to make her feel uncomfortable. Now, Katy, not to sound egotistical, but did Cal talk about me at all?"

"A fine question. Would you by any chance mean about this whole book business?"

"I would. It was pretty creepy, let me tell you. You didn't remember mentioning it, and neither did anyone else. Cal did a good job reassuring me, but still. A spirit talking through my friends without their knowing it? Well, I just wonder what I'm getting myself into."

"Everyone on a quest wonders that. It's part of the process. But you have people who understand helping you. Especially—"

"Sir Caliman?" I smiled. "Yes, I'm lucky to have him. I'm happy for you, Katy."

"It's about time, isn't it?" she grinned.

"No one deserves it more. Uh-oh," I added in an undertone. "They spotted us. Stephen is headed this way."

"At least *she's* not coming," Katy muttered.

I stole a glance at Jenny. She was looking over with a glacial expression. I almost laughed but bit my lip.

Stephen was cheerfulness itself. "Hello, ladies," he said. "A beautiful day, isn't it?"

It was gray and drizzly outside, but Katy answered enthusiastically, "It sure is!"

"Lily, how are you feeling?" was Stephen's next question. "Everything okay?"

I couldn't suppress a surge of annoyance. "I'm fine, thanks. I only killed two people yesterday. Dr. Carson said howling at the moon is definitely helping."

"All right, all right. I was just asking. No offense."

"How is Sandy?"

"Better, much better," Stephen said happily. "We located the source of the bleeding and were able to stop it. Jenny and I are here celebrating."

"That's great! Congratulations."

"We make a good team." Stephen glanced back over at Jenny. "Well, it was nice to see you. Talk to you soon."

After we said our goodbyes, Katy clapped her hands to the sides of her face. "Did I just hear Stephen Mallory modestly sharing credit with someone? Can it be?"

"The little Thompson girl means a lot to him. It was touch and go with her for a while. I'm so glad she's better."

"So am I, but I'm still amazed. Could this be love?"

"Probably." My tone was gloomy. "For you, for Stephen, for everybody but me." Katy looked sad, and I immediately felt guilty. "I'm sorry. Who am I to rain on the parade? I'm glad for both of you, honestly."

"Well, it's not like Kent is dead. There's real hope for you, Lily. I, for one, still think you'll end up together."

Her cell phone rang, and I saw her face light up even before she said, "Hi, Cal! I'm fine. I'm having lunch with Lily. Hold on a minute, and I'll go outside. It's so noisy in here." *Sorry*, she mouthed to me.

I waved my hand as she rose. "Go on. I'll just eat." But I simply picked at the food left on my plate. It was hard to stop thinking about Kent. *Will we really end up together?* I wanted that so much, but the difficulties refused to go away. I let my mind toy with the idea of running off to join him in England, abandoning all my responsibilities and dreaming of him welcoming me with open arms. I'd dreamt it often enough, but I'd always come back to the cold, hard truth: *I just...can't.*

Katy reappeared, all smiles. "He's taking me out to dinner at Morigeau's. Imagine! No one has ever treated me to a place like that."

"You've definitely moved up in the world. Their appetizers cost more than the dinners at other restaurants. Lucky girl. And I'll be sitting at home with my tuna noodle casserole."

"Poor baby. I'll be crying right into my soup. If you loan me some jewelry, I'll bring you a doggy bag."

"It's yours. Come over before you leave and pick something out."

"Thanks." She rose from her seat. "I'd better be getting back to work. Are you finished?"

"Definitely. I'm not staying here alone so Stephen feels compelled to invite me to their table."

When I got home, I made my daily call to the hospital. My mother, they said, was fine—eating well, sleeping well and interacting with other patients. She'd told them all about her daughter, who was almost done with graduate school and engaged to a doctor. That idea remained frozen in her mind, and she couldn't think past it. I thanked them and hung up, then burst into a flood of tears.

Cleo came and curled up beside me on the couch. Everyone kept telling me I was handling everything so well, but they couldn't see the anguish I felt deep inside. I let myself cry it out for a while. It was all that new business of opening my mind and delving into my psyche, coupled with the fact that Stephen had a new girlfriend and Katy was spending more and more time with Cal. Life kept moving on. *Will it move on for Kent too?*

Finally I made myself get up and do something. I vacuumed the living room rug and dusted all the furniture. That made me feel better, so I tackled the kitchen next. When everything was gleaming, I was too tired to be sad anymore. I picked a light mystery novel out of the bookcase. I soon became so engrossed in it that the ringing of the telephone made me jump. I reached across Cleo to pick it up.

"Lily, hi. It's Cal. How's everything going?"

I smiled. "Are you psychic or something? Actually, I'm not having the best day."

"I'm sorry. What's wrong?"

It was too long of a tale to tell, so I just said, "The usual. I'm trying to assimilate all these new experiences. It's like starting college over again."

"I know, believe me. It's never easy for any of us. But it really is better than shoving it all down beneath the surface. Then it just bubbles and finally erupts like a volcano."

I already felt as if I'd erupted several times, but I didn't tell him that. "What's up with you?"

"Don't worry. It's nothing to do with the paranormal. I just wanted to know what Katy's favorite flower is. I'm taking her out to dinner, and I want to surprise her with a bouquet."

"How sweet. She'll love that. She loves white roses."

"Thanks. And, um…"

"Now for the paranormal?"

"Well, we were just planning a little trip on Saturday. We're going over to Morrisville Park for a picnic. We'd love for you to come."

Saturday was supposed to be another beautiful Indian summer day, and I loved the park. "All right, thanks. What can I bring?"

"Whatever you like, but your company is the most important thing."

"You're such a gentleman, Cal. You and Katy have a great time tonight."

"Katy and great times go together naturally. And if you can make it, tomorrow night is a good time for the rest of us to get together. Jo has come up with some interesting information about Rose."

My curiosity was definitely piqued. "Okay. I'll be there. Seven thirty? That's fine."

I hung up thinking about all the flowers Kent had given me. My longing for him was sharp. Whether it would increase or lessen my sadness I didn't know, but I had to sketch him. Getting out my paper and charcoal pencils, I drew his fine-boned face, beautiful gray eyes and dark hair.

I was starting to fill in the outline of his neck and shoulders when a very strange thing happened. The pencil started moving without my guidance. Some force was pushing it into the creation of pictures my brain had no part in forming. Rose was sitting on a bench, a shawl draped around her, wearing a crown of flowers. Next to her was a muscular, handsome man with black hair and a beard.

Vitality leapt from my pencil to their figures like a spark. Lying at their feet was the wolf, stretched out with his head on his paws, and in Rose's lap was a book, a heavy volume bound in leather. Then words appeared. I didn't even know what I was writing until my hand had stopped. At the bottom of the paper were sentences in a script that was not my own:

I also have loved and lost. You must find the book. Give it to the seeker of knowledge. He will understand what must be done.

Rose! Rose has been behind all this. I felt a chill along my skin. I knew she was only trying to communicate, but it was uncomfortable being hijacked. I stared at my portrait of Kent. *What will he say to all this?*

"I also have loved and lost." Is that why she feels a kinship with me? But Rose had her husband, and Kent was very much alive. I hadn't lost him yet. *This seems to be about the book.*

The "seeker of knowledge" has to be Cal. So why can't she just tell him where the book was? It would be so much easier. I'd listened to everyone in the group explain how their abilities varied, how nothing was written in stone in the field, how the right frequency had to be found. But I wasn't sure I really understood it.

Still, if it's left up to me and that book will give the world valuable information, I have a responsibility, don't I? I closed my eyes. *Rose, where is it?* I sat with the pencil in my hand, waiting. But there was no answering voice nor any movement. Rose could not tell me yet.

I suddenly felt exhausted. I went to take a nap and did not wake up until I heard the front doorbell ringing. Glancing at the clock, I saw that it was after five. I shifted Cleocatra over and climbed out of bed.

Katy was waiting outside, running her eyes over my rumpled figure. "Were you sleeping? Sorry. I'm here for some jewelry, remember?"

"Sure. Come on in." I yawned and rubbed my eyes. "I only meant to lie down for a little while, but time got away from me."

"Who can blame you? Your mind's been on overload lately. Are you okay?"

"Yes, I'm fine." I wasn't going to tell her or Cal about the automatic drawing and writing—at least not yet. *Let them have their evening of fun unaware.* "What dress are you going to wear?"

"The black velvet with the tastefully revealing neckline. That's why I need something dramatic to set it off—like your pearls or maybe that onyx choker. What do you think?"

"Hmm. Let's go have a look."

We went through my drawer and finally decided on a necklace with three rows of green beads. They were strung on finely filigreed gold mesh, giving it a lovely Victorian effect. I had earrings to match, and Katy tried everything on with the enthusiasm of a girl going to her first prom. "You'll be absolutely stunning," I told her, "and you'll have a great time."

"If I can manage not to spill anything, I'll be happy. Thanks for helping me out."

I gave her a hug. "You're more than welcome. Now go home and prepare to dazzle."

"I won't have to be sophisticated and order snails, will I?"

"I'm not sure. Let me check the *Fancy Dining Rule Book*." I flipped open the mystery novel on my nightstand. "Let's see. No tripping. No talking loudly about anyone's medical problems. No staring at any famous fellow diners. Oh, here we are…seems ordering of snails is strictly optional."

"Thank goodness. I don't want to do anything to embarrass Cal. I can just see this necklace falling off into the soup."

"You'd better not see that! Go on…and don't forget my doggy bag."

I watched her leave, hoping she'd love the experience. The place seemed very empty after she had gone.

Chapter Nine

The following evening saw all of us back at Cal's house. The only person missing was, to my relief, Yvette; she apparently had to work.

Jo was excited by the information she'd found. After we were all settled in with drinks and bowls of snack food, she pulled out a notebook. "I did a lot of reading and talked to the Morrisville historian. Their records go all the way back to 1680. Of course, there are a lot of second- and third-hand accounts—mostly gossip—and missing material. One can never know all the facts, but this is what I came up with." She readied a pen to tick off the items.

"Apparently there was a town where the park is now—Woodville. Thomas Woodbine's father, Amos, founded it with a group of settlers from England. The family was very prominent. They had a big house in the middle of town."

She turned a page. "Amos had a daughter, Irene, and two sons, Thomas and Jacob. There was a bit of a scandal when Thomas married Rose Adams. She came from a poor family, but she was very beautiful. She had spurned the advances of several suitors, so it wasn't surprising when people assumed she was only after Thomas's money. He stood to inherit the house and a lot of land, leaving Jacob well enough off, though with considerably less than his big brother."

I reached for a handful of popcorn as Jo continued.

"Rose and Thomas had a house built on the outskirts of town. Thomas was rather sickly, so Jacob did a lot of work for him. Well, eventually Thomas succumbed to his disease—probably pleurisy—and then Rose married Jacob. There must have been a lot of talk about that."

"Typical," Amy said indignantly. "The whole town was probably jealous of her for being beautiful and rich."

"And knowing that, Rose likely didn't make much of an effort to mix with them," Cal remarked. "She preferred to run her household and taking care of animals. That, in itself, was enough to make her stand out. There was no PETA in those days. Animals were considered as nothing more than livestock or tools, like the plow and the axe. If they got hurt, they were slaughtered for food."

"And Rose nursed anything that came her way back to health. Plus, she had a wolf for a pet," Amy said.

With a shiver, I imagined my Cleo having to live in those days. "It didn't pay to be different back then."

"A lot of the time, it still doesn't," Derek said. "The human race is pretty conservative."

"Well, to top it all off, smallpox broke out," Jo went on. "About a fourth of the town was wiped out in the epidemic. Shortly after that, Rose herself was killed. Lightning struck her house—a sign from God, of course—and she died in the fire. That was the official verdict anyway. Jacob died shortly afterwards in a hunting accident."

Everyone was silent for a minute. "So that's how they left it to history," Cal said at last. "God's righteous anger killed the evil witch. It wasn't that a crazy mob executed an innocent woman in the most horrendous way possible. No wonder people feel uneasy when they look at her portrait. They can sense the fear, injustice and hatred, and there's nothing to attach it to but that beautiful face. Poor Rose."

"We've got to try and help her find peace," Jo stated. "What's the best way to do it?"

"Well," Amy suggested, "the original Woodbine house is still there, preserved by the park. It's a museum now."

"That's where the portrait came from," I said. "Jacob must have saved it and hidden it in his old home."

"Perfect. We'll go there. It's the closest we'll get to being able to get to Rose. Maybe we can reach her then." Cal looked excited.

"Do the records mention any other members of the Woodbine family, Jo?" Derek asked. "It would help if we could find a living relative to participate."

"There were some cousins. They inherited the land, but they seem to have died out. I couldn't trace them past 1720. The house and the town graveyard are all that remain of Woodville now."

"Funny," Amy mused. "All the times I've been there, I hardly ever noticed them. I just walk the trails and go to see the waterfalls. Every year my friends take a picture of me standing on the same bridge."

"We can check the cemetery," Derek said. "We might find the rest of the Woodbines, but Rose won't be there. They wouldn't have buried her in holy ground. They probably just scattered her ashes and hoped everyone would forget her."

"Well, thanks to Lily, that won't happen. She's gotten some more information." Cal went on to explain about the book. "We don't know what's in it, but it must be very important to Rose. I think it's the key to ending her suffering. We have to find it."

Since I had told him about the message from Rose calling him the "seeker of knowledge," Cal had been on a mission. For someone who succeeded at everything he tried, he was determined to get the book and harvest its wisdom. He felt it could help mankind.

"Maybe we can go to the house and have a séance," Amy offered.

"I can't see the park authorities welcoming that." Derek made a face. "But just being there should provide a lot of energy."

"All right," Cal agreed, "but let's get over to the gallery for now."

This time we took one car. There was a strong wind blowing across the rain-washed streets, sending clouds of leaves swirling everywhere. They hit the car with loud slapping sounds. It was a night right out of a horror movie: five people in a storm, riding to a rendezvous with a witch.

But of course she wasn't one, I reminded myself. *Rose was only an innocent victim of cruel gossip and torment.* Still, I couldn't help but feel anxious. I hadn't had as much experience as the rest of the group. It was unsettling to open myself up to a tormented woman who'd been dead for 300 years.

While the others chattered away, I thought about the book. *What will it turn out to be, and how will we react to whatever's in it? Could it possibly still exist, hidden away somewhere? What will it reveal about Rose, and why is it so important to her?* My thoughts danced around like the leaves. It was a heavy responsibility, knowing that a spirit's rest might depend on us. I didn't know if I would ever get used to that.

When we reached the gallery, we all walked quickly with our heads down against the wind. Even inside, we could hear it howling. I turned on every light in the place, and then we gathered around Rose.

Her painted face looked expectant, as if she'd been waiting for us. We all stood silently for a minute, greeting her.

Jo asked, "Shall I go first?"

We nodded agreement, and Jo reached out to touch the frame. After a while, a puzzled look crossed her face. "I'm getting nothing. There's no response at all."

"Let me try." Amy took her place, but the result was the same. "She doesn't seem to want to talk tonight."

"But she must." Cal frowned. "She obviously wants us to know about the book."

He didn't ask me, but there wasn't any other answer. Without speaking, I stepped up to the picture. Immediately a charge went through me. I saw Rose seated at a table, her pet wolf at her feet, writing in a large book. I could hear her breathing, the crackling of wood in the fireplace, the scratching of the quill pen on the paper. I could feel her excitement, the power and joy she felt in the words, the knowledge of how important they were.

She worked quickly but carefully, and I watched her for some time. At last she stopped, blotted the final page and looked up at me. "You must find this," she said. "They never destroyed it, for we hid it well. It is important—even more important than my life. It contains all the wisdom I have gathered. Within are the plants and the flowers for healing, the quantities and the mixtures to use. It teaches how to treat both man and beast and tells of lore and legends. The book will bring much good to your people."

"Where is it, Rose? Where did you hide it?"

Her eyes, so alive even on canvas, were almost painfully brilliant, looking through time into mine. "It is—"

But suddenly the wolf growled and leapt to its feet. Rose jumped too, hastily concealing the heavy tome under a mahogany cabinet.

Then the contact was broken. I drew in a deep breath and opened my eyes to find everyone staring at me.

"You reached her!" Cal exclaimed.

"Yes." I felt lightheaded and made my way to a chair. "Just give me a minute."

"Of course. Do you want a drink or something?" Cal asked.

I nodded. "Water please. There's some in the refrigerator in back."

No one spoke while Cal went to fetch it.

I gulped down the cool liquid appreciatively. "Wow. That takes a lot out of you."

"Yes it does. You just sit and rest. Take your time. Tell us if you need anything."

I nodded again.

They all had the good grace to move around the gallery and look at the artwork so I wouldn't feel pressured.

When I was better, I said, "She showed me the book."

Everyone turned and came back to stand around me.

"Could you see her, like before?" Derek asked.

"Yes, it was just like being there. She was writing, and then she spoke to me. She told me the book concerns medicine and folklore. She said she'd put all her knowledge in it, and it was more important than her life. She hid it so it was never discovered, and now she wants us to benefit from it. It's all about healing."

"Healing for us and for her," Jo said. "She only ever wanted to help, and they killed her for it. The same thing happened to many wise women. The establishment was afraid of them, so they accused them of witchcraft and got rid of them."

"Well, at least this is one wrong we can help right," Cal pronounced. "Rose can endow us with her legacy and be cleared of witchcraft. It's too late for her mortal life but not for her soul. Where's the book, Lily?"

I hated to let them down, but I had to. "I don't know," I confessed. "Something happened before she could tell me. Someone was coming, and she shoved the book under a cabinet. She wasn't able to show me where it ended up."

There was a murmur of disappointment. "Well," Cal said, "she's doing the best she can. And so are you, Lily. You've been amazing."

"Why do you suppose she only made contact with me?" I asked. "Both Derek and Jo could read her before."

"I don't know," Cal answered. "There are no hard and fast rules. She seems to have singled you out."

Great. So it's going to be up to me.

Cal seemed to know what I was thinking. "Before we go, why don't we practice some more protection exercises? We can all help."

And so, for the next hour, I got another dose of their collective wisdom. I called down the light and let it flow through me. I focused on pleasant thoughts when negative ones threatened me. I centered myself in a calm place inside, and I learned to disassociate from stress. I felt tired but very relaxed by the time we were through.

"There," Cal said with satisfaction. "Keep practicing and read the books I gave you. You're going to be fine."

Chapter Ten

When I got home, I decided to reinforce the lessons I was learning. I thought of Rose.

Death had made her spirit restless, and if I were to help her find peace, I'd have to experience the pain also. Fully accepting this gift meant learning to distance myself from that pain. I was beginning to see that it was possible with the help of Cal and his friends, but I was far from feeling fully confident. But the satisfaction of knowing I could help to set a soul free was a powerful incentive.

I sat down and started thinking about my own life. Images of love and warmth I had known passed before my eyes. I saw my father beaming with pride while I accepted a school prize for a drawing. I remembered my mother staying up all night to make favors for my birthday party. Katy making me laugh with her wisecracks. Stephen taking me out for banana splits whenever I got depressed. I thought of Cleocatra, who owned me as much as I owned her. And of course, there was Kent. I relived our first date and our first kiss as fireworks soared in the sky above us. I could feel his embrace and hear him telling me he loved me. I was truly blessed to have so much light in my soul.

I began saying over and over in my head, like a prayer: *Daddy, Mom, Kent, Katy, Stephen, Cleo…* I could repeat that mantra whenever I started to feel overwhelmed. I could never forget who *I* was, no matter who else's soul I looked into. I could always mentally bring myself back home, where I was safe.

I got up and walked around the rooms I rented, suddenly seeing them through new eyes. The living room was done in cream and light green, with my grandparents' clock and antique coffee table. It had a long sofa with lots of pillows and a comfortable overstuffed chair where I usually sat. A bookcase took up nearly all of one wall, and it was full to overflowing. Katy joked that I had more volumes about the ancient world than the lost library of Alexandria.

Most of my books did concern Egypt, but I had other favorites too. My very first book, *Go, Dog. Go*, inscribed: *To Lily, Love Mommy and Daddy. Merry Christmas*. And *The Wind in the Willows*, a precious gift from my father for my eighth birthday. He'd read a chapter to me every night, using different voices for each character. I took both of them down and leafed through them with a smile. My childhood was preserved between their pages like magic.

Next was the kitchen, a wonderful honey yellow with marble countertops and dark oak cabinets. Admittedly, I wasn't much of a cook and didn't spend a lot of time in there, but I did eat at the little round table with the two high-backed chairs. The small adjoining dining room was only used for more formal occasions. It had a china cabinet, but instead of dishes, that cabinet held a host of Egyptian curios. Models of sphinxes, pyramids, famous pharaohs, temples, gods and goddesses crowded the shelves. The latest addition was a turquoise scarab that Kent had sent from the British Museum.

I let my mind dwell on him. He was over six feet tall, and when we hugged, he rested his cheek on the top of my head. It was a simple gesture but one I found to be incredibly tender.

He had a dry sense of humor and wasn't afraid to laugh at me or himself. A lover of opera, he sang in Italian with great enthusiasm, albeit with a terrible voice. He was a scientist enthralled with his subject; he never stopped trying to convert me. We were both sensible people caught up in an uncharacteristic whirlwind romance. I loved him so much.

Before my thoughts could turn bittersweet, I walked down the hall that led to my office. I had a huge oak desk, every drawer crammed with papers and art supplies. My easel seemed to look at me reproachfully. It had been a while since I'd painted anything. The light was wonderful in there, with floor-to-ceiling windows and hardwood floors. I always papered them liberally before my palette came out. My computer rested in there as well, with its Johnny Depp screensaver. Kent had heaped scorn upon it and had tried to replace the picture with Etruscans more than once.

I passed into the bedroom. It was a lemony chiffon color, feminine but not fussy. I couldn't stand fussy. The plain curtains matched the Laura Ashley comforter. Cleo had a bed in there too, but it was much more likely that she'd end up sleeping on top of my head in the middle of the night.

The dresser was filled with photographs and souvenirs, including a program from an American Ballet Theatre presentation signed by my favorite dancer, Wendy Potemki. I had waited by the stage door for over two hours to obtain the treasure, while Stephen complained the whole time.

This is my home, my still point. The new awareness of its beauty impressed itself upon my mind. I was pleased to know that I'd manufactured a powerful shield that would serve me well in the future.

I kicked off my shoes and was sitting on the bed when Cleo came in. She was purring, and I picked her up to hug her. "Did you miss me, sweet pea?"

She purred louder and looked at me expectantly, then wriggled out of my arms. Five seconds later the doorbell rang. Cleo raced off, and I followed her reluctantly.

There stood Stephen, who scooped up the ecstatic cat and said, "Hi girls. Have you got time for a visit?"

"Sure." In spite of my fatigue, I could see that something was bothering him. "Come on in."

He sat down on the sofa with Cleo in his lap. "I'm sorry to come by so late, but you weren't home earlier." His tone sounded faintly accusing, but I let it pass.

"I was at a friend's house. What's wrong, Stephen?"

He sighed. "It's Ellen. I got another letter begging for money. She's in Thailand now and doesn't have enough to get home."

Ellen was forever traveling the world to find the meaning of life. As far as I knew, she was no closer to her goal than she'd ever been. She was the archetypal free spirit, as different from her brother as night from day. But then again, she'd never had to assume the burden of caring for and protecting the family from an alcoholic father. Her reaction was to run; Stephen's was to become imminently practical and take charge. He felt responsible for Ellen the way he felt responsible for his patients and for me.

I wanted to say, *"Tell her to grow up and think seriously for a change,"* But I didn't. Instead I remarked, "You can't afford to keep doing this. You're not a rich doctor yet. And anyway, what good does it do to go on bailing her out? It's not like she learns anything from it."

"I know, I know. But she never listens to me. God knows I've tried to talk some sense into her."

I could well imagine that and the way Ellen would respond. "Why don't you send her the money," I suggested, "on the condition that she stay home for at least six months? She could try to find a job and live in one place for a while. If she won't do it, you've got to stick to your guns and not give her another cent."

"But, Lily, I have to know she's all right. I can't let her go wandering off and end up stranded who knows where."

"Stephen, she's a grown woman. She's smart and tough. She can look after herself. It's not your job to take care of her. You've done more than enough for her. I know it doesn't seem like it, because you feel you have to take care of everything, but you don't. You're going to help her by getting her home. After that, it's up to her. Please try to realize that."

He still looked troubled, but he nodded his head. I went over to the sofa and gave him a hug. Cleocatra's expression was blissful. *Mommy and Daddy are together again.*

"How would you like a game of Parcheesi?" I asked. "It's nice and mindless, and you always feel good when you beat me."

Stephen actually smiled. "You know I'm going to send you back if I get the chance."

"I know. I did pick up somewhere along the line that you're a little competitive."

I got out the board, and we sat at the kitchen table, drinking wine and throwing the dice. As always, Stephen won, but I didn't mind. It was relaxing, and I enjoyed myself.

"How are things going with Jenny?" I kept my voice deliberately casual.

"Fine." His eyes lit up. "You should see her in surgery. She has the quickest hands and the coolest head I've ever seen. She can tie off a vein in nothing flat."

"No kidding? Well, that's a wonderful skill, I guess, but I hope I *don't* ever have to see it."

"And she's a runner too. We went all the way around the reservoir at Dobb's Hill this morning. We're thinking of entering the fall 5K."

"You've certainly got a lot in common. Aha! Doubles." I moved my piece and took an extra turn. In the first throes of love, I had jogged with Stephen a grand total of three times. I admired his healthy lifestyle, but I found myself unable to follow it.

"She told me I'm the most interesting person she's ever met." He said this as if he couldn't quite believe it himself.

I wanted to reach out and chuck him under the chin the way one would a child. "You *are* interesting. You have great depth of character."

Cleocatra, who had curled up under the table, sneezed.

I laughed. "Cleo agrees."

Stephen bent down and scratched her head. "I've missed you."

I wasn't sure if he was addressing me or the cat. "We've missed you too."

He straightened up. "Jenny's beautiful, isn't she?"

Does he expect my approval? "Oh? You noticed that in between the veins and the running, did you?"

He grinned. "Actually, I noticed it as soon as I saw her."

"Dr. Mallory, there's hope for you yet!"

After four games, we called it a night. As I was packing up the pieces, Stephen caught my hand, leaned over and kissed me. "Thanks," he said.

"You're welcome. I'm always here for you, Stephen. You know that."

"I know…and the same goes for me."

After he left, I got ready for bed, thinking of that warm, gentle kiss. It had felt so right, devoid of passion but filled with love. I checked the computer to see if Kent had written, but there was nothing.

I didn't take my medicine. I had difficulty getting to sleep in spite of my fatigue, but I was determined to break free from those pills. At last I fell into an uneasy slumber, and that was when I had the dream.

I call it a "dream," yet I had the strange sense of being awake. I was lying in my bed, and suddenly a white mist seemed to be filling the room. I stared into it, and the face of Rose appeared.

"Lily," she said, "I have come to tell you a great secret. You desire to know where the book is hidden. Look, and I will show you."

A house solidified out of the swirling mist. I could see Rose walking away from it, towards a grove of trees, carrying an iron box. A cape streamed out behind her. A man accompanied her, Jacob. She was holding his hand, and I got a clear sense of the love between them. A gray wolf followed behind. The little procession stopped in front of a towering oak tree with two large boulders on either side.

"We will dig here," Rose said. "It is well marked."

Jacob produced a shovel and slid it into the earth.

When the hole was deep enough, Rose placed the box down into it, muttering under her breath the whole time. "These spells will protect it." She stood up. "Only someone of the true blood will be able to uncover it." She took a knife from Jacob and marked a symbol on the tree. Then she turned from the past and looked directly at me. "Lily, you must get the book." Her tone had turned commanding now. "It is all that matters. You cannot deny me. It is your duty. We are alike, you and I. The same blood runs in our veins."

I gasped.

Rose nodded. "Oh yes. Where do you think you received your gift? It has come down through the ages from mother to daughter. Some ignore it, afraid of the possibilities. Some embrace it and bend the world to their will. The unfortunate few who are discovered, as I was, are called witches and destroyed."

A spasm of pain crossed her face, and for a moment, she faltered. Jacob squeezed her hand.

"But I was too powerful to be erased." Her voice gained strength once more. "I have kept my consciousness alive in the dark night, for I knew one day you would come. Find the book and retrieve all my knowledge. I will share it with you. It is your birthright. What wonders we could work together!" She leaned towards me in excitement. "I am skilled at healing. We could bring your mother back from where she wanders, make her whole again. You can be joined with your true love, as I was joined with mine. Think on it and do not be afraid. Only the ignorant despise us. You are part of the sisterhood, Lily. Be a credit to them." Then she turned suddenly, as if she heard someone coming. "I must go. Do not forsake me!"

Her image wavered and then disappeared.

I awoke sweating and with a pounding headache. I lay trying to remember what I'd seen.

Rose's words astonished me. *What did she mean by "the same blood?" Could she really have been a relative of mine?* I remembered nothing of her in the family history. *Tomorrow I will have to check with my aunt. Is that why I have psychic ability? Because I have a witch as an ancestor?*

The shocking revelation kept me awake for a long time. When I finally fell back to sleep, it seemed only moments later that the alarm went off. I reached for it with a groan.

It was nine o'clock, and I was supposed to be at Cal's apartment by ten. I reluctantly dragged myself out of bed and got ready.

Chapter Eleven

The first thing I did was call my aunt. Luckily for me, she was on her way to the grocery store and in a hurry as well, but she had time to tell me the name of Rose Adams Woodbine wasn't at all familiar. She remembered Cowns and Whitehalls from the eighteenth century, but without delving deeper into the research, she couldn't give me any more information.

I put on jeans and my favorite green shirt, because the forecast was for sunny skies and a temperature in the low seventies. I tied my hair up in a ponytail and looked for my sneakers. One was right next to the bed where I'd left it, but I couldn't see the other one anywhere.

I went into the living room where Cleocatra liked to hide things behind the sofa, but there was nothing. Next I tried the laundry room, and sure enough, in between the washer and the dryer, there it was. How the cat knew when I was planning to be gone the whole day was beyond me, but it was her way of protesting. I went into the kitchen and found her sitting in front of her food bowl, regarding me sadly.

"Oh, don't give me that," I said as I put out her Fancy Fixins. "I know you'll gobble all of it up as soon as I leave. See? I crumbled one of your bon-bons on top. You'll be just fine until I get back."

I bent down to rub her, and she let out a pitiful little mew. "See you later, sweet pea. You be a good girl."

I put a carefully wrapped picture in the back of the car, planning to stop at the gallery on my way to the picnic.

Carolyn was in her office eating breakfast when I arrived. "Hi, Lily. Would you like a bagel?"

"No thanks. I just had a very healthy meal of cinnamon toast and Diet Cherry Coke. I'm actually on my way to Morrisville. I came to bring you another picture to replace Isis."

"Ooh! Let me see."

I took off the paper to display Thoth, the ibis-headed god of wisdom and one of my favorites. I had painted him with his lunar disc and crescent, since he was closely identified with the moon. He was the messenger of the gods and the patron saint of scribes, the one who recorded the results at the weighing of the heart ceremony after death. That was the scene I had put him in, standing before the scales of justice.

Carolyn was delighted. "It's exquisite! I'm sure he won't be here for long. Let's go put him on display right by the door. Grab that easel, will you?"

Thoth was duly installed, and Carolyn stood back to admire him. "There. Perfect. We don't want to put him too close to the witch."

"Carolyn, we know who she is now." I filled her in on Rose's history. "We really think they burned her alive."

Carolyn's gentle face registered horror. "Because she loved animals and married a wealthy man? What an age to live in!"

"Conditions are not much better for a lot of women in the world today." I sighed. "When does her portrait have to be back in Morrisville?"

"Oh, it's on indefinite loan. Perhaps it made them as uneasy as it makes me. The tragedy comes through it, I suppose. It draws people, but they seem to be almost frightened by it as well—except for your friend Cal, that is. I think he could stare at it for hours"

"Has he been in here?" I asked in surprise.

"Yes, two or three times. He has a notebook and scribbles things down. I haven't seen anyone else from your group of friends though."

"Hmm. I'll have to ask him about it. Right now I'd better be off to pick up some brownies, my contribution to the day's feast. Thanks so much, Carolyn." I kissed her on the cheek. "I'll see you later."

I fetched the goodies from the bakery and then drove to Cal's apartment. Jo, Derek and Amy were already waiting, but there was no sign of Yvette.

"She's made herself scarce lately," Amy confided. "I don't think she's very happy with these new developments. She sort of looks on Cal as her own private property."

I was glad she wasn't there, but I loved the company of everyone else. We were making a business and pleasure trip out of it, having a picnic and going over Rose's home ground.

It was a lovely drive through the changing trees into the park. We saw several deer grazing in the long grass. After a couple miles, the flat land changed to narrower, rocky outcroppings as we drove alongside a gorge.

We parked at an overlook and got out to gaze at the magnificent view. A concrete dam had been built to hold the waters back, but after a dry summer, the river was barely flowing. An aerie of hawks circled lazily overhead, weaving in and out in an elaborate dance. Several people were taking pictures, and I snapped a couple too. Then we got back in our car and followed a road that dropped steadily downwards into a valley.

"Watch for directions now," Cal said. "It shouldn't be far."

And it wasn't. We soon passed a wooden signpost pointing to Tea Table Rock, a huge, flat stone with picnic tables all around it. We piled out of the car and unpacked our food.

Everyone had contributed something, and it was an eclectic menu: roast beef and chicken subs, cream cheese and pimento sandwiches, deviled eggs, potato salad, and even peanut butter and jelly. Jo had made chocolate chip cookies, and I was biting into one when Cal said, "Look! Fairy stones!"

All eyes followed where his finger pointed, at a heap of large pebbles on the ground. "What's special about them?" I asked.

"My mom told me the fair folk collect them. They lay them in circles and dance around inside them under the moonlight. They like them because they're polished and smooth. I used to spend a lot of time searching for the right ones to tempt the fairies into my back yard."

"Did it ever work?"

"Once. I found them arranged in a circle, and I was sure there'd been a dance. I was beyond thrilled. The grass was flattened too, as if their feet had worn it down. I'm sure Mom did it to make me happy, even though she denied it."

"Sounds like my dad," I said wistfully. "He went along with every crazy thing I ever thought up. When he mowed the lawn, he always left a corner where some mushrooms grew. I was convinced that fairies lived under them. I used to crumble up cookies so they'd have something to eat."

"I never thought about magical creatures." Amy reached for a brownie. "My spirit friends were more interesting."

Cal pulled out a pocket knife and carved an old man's face out of an apple. With the sun shining down and everyone laughing and talking, I felt happy. Those people accepted me for who I was, and I was comfortable with them.

I'd wanted a relaxed meal, so I'd waited to share my news, but by the time we were finished, I was bursting to tell it. While helping to pack up the basket, I announced, "I had a dream about Rose last night."

"Well," Cal said, "don't keep us in suspense. What was it?"

I paused dramatically. "She showed me where the book is."

Excited exclamations broke out around me.

"The book!"

"Really?"

"What happened?"

Cal took me by the shoulders. "Lily, how could you hold out on us? This is fantastic. Tell us everything!"

I related every detail I could remember. "The problem is that the house is long gone. Who knows if the trees are even still there? But I get the feeling that she thinks we can find the place, or she wouldn't have bothered to come to me."

"You're right," Cal replied. "She's guiding you. I hope everyone feels like a good hike, because we've got some ground to cover."

"Cal, do you know how many acres this park has?" Jo asked. "Where do we start?"

"Well, we know where the town was. We'll go find the old Woodbine house first. It will be interesting to see what we pick up in there. Then we'll know where *not* to search. Rose's house was on the fringes of the town. I notice that most of the trees around here are maples, elms and birches. We'll be on the lookout for oaks. And let's just hope those boulders are still there."

I had my doubts after all those years, but I did believe Rose would guide me. I said lightly to Cal, "Your druid powers ought to lead you right to the oak trees," but he didn't seem to hear me. He was gathering the rest of our things almost feverishly, clearly anxious to get the book. I myself was a little afraid of what might be found in it.

We got back into the car and drove a few miles to the marker stating: *Former Site of Woodville, est. 1680.* The house soon loomed up before us.

It was a honey-colored, two-and-a-half-story, box-like wooden structure. The top slightly overhung the bottom, and there was a chimney off to one side. It had a gray slate roof and many windows, staring out at us like eyes from the past.

We parked the car and walked up the front steps into another world. It seemed as if time had stood still in that place. We were in a foyer with polished hardwood floors that gleamed. A coat tree was on our left, and a marble bust on a pediment occupied the space to our right.

We signed the guest ledger, and a cheerful guide informed us that we'd just missed the tour. "But feel free to look around and don't hesitate to ask if you have any questions."

We thanked her and moved forward. The foyer narrowed into a passageway that led to a staircase, but we decided to explore the ground floor first. We followed a branch into a parlor with a lovely tiled fireplace, complete with a huge mantel. On it stood a carriage clock and candlesticks in intricately worked silver holders.

Overhead hung a portrait of a man whom I knew was Amos Woodbine. He had a full wig of white hair and an imperious, determined look about him. As I stared at his likeness, a sudden feeling of hatred came over me, so strong that it made me tremble. I gasped, and Cal put his arm around my shoulders. "What is it, Lily? What are you feeling?"

"I-I need to leave this room please."

We made our way to the other side of the main passageway and into the dining area. There, a long oak table with a white cloth runner was laid with a service for eight people.

I concentrated on the pewter dishes and the dried flowers in the center, breathing deeply and trying to clear my mind. The others waited in respectful silence until I was calm enough to say, "That was Amos Woodbine. He ruled this house like his own private kingdom. How must he have felt when both of his sons defied him and married a woman of such inferior rank and quality? He despised Rose and feared her. I believe it was he who turned people against her. He stirred the feelings that she was a witch. Rose's father-in-law was the main cause of her death."

Jo rubbed my back soothingly. "Does anyone else sense this?"

They shook their heads. "Not in such detail," Derek said, "but there is a heavy feeling, as if the atmosphere is pressing down on us. It's unnerving. 'All torment, trouble, wonder and amazement. Inhabits here…some heavenly power guide us. Out of this fearful country!'"

"I seem to be all right," Cal said. "If you want to go outside and get some fresh air, Lily, I'll go on."

"No." I was determined. "I came here to listen to Rose, and I'm going to." I squared my shoulders. "I'm not picking up anything in here. Let's check out the library."

In any other house, the library would have been a cozy room. It was paneled in dark wood, with rugs scattered on the floor. A small fireplace was topped by a mantel decorated with glass figurines. A sideboard stood with a selection of empty bottles that would have brimmed with spirits when the residents were alive.

There were three more portraits on the wall. Two were of young men, clearly resembling Woodbine, but with softer countenances and less severe clothing. One had curly blond hair, and the other was darkly handsome.

"Thomas and Jacob," I said. "I feel love and passion when I look at Jacob." I paused. "Rose belonged to him, body and soul."

The other picture was of a woman. She was also young, with a sweet and gentle face that seemed somehow familiar. A sense of sadness enveloped me, although in the picture she was smiling and appeared quite content.

"This must be Irene before tragedy destroyed her family. Poor girl."

I stepped away and looked at the shelves lined with musty old books, all educational or religious. I felt a chill when I saw a volume on witchcraft. That was the time period when the trials at Salem were taking place and hysteria was at its height. For a brief moment, I could see flames again and hear screaming. I put my hand up to my forehead. "I'm sorry, but I have to go. Rose knew such misery in this house, and it's still here. I'll wait outside."

They all offered to come with me, but I insisted on being by myself. Once out of the house, I felt better. I walked down the stone driveway to the trees that fringed the property. A flat rock made a perfect place to sit and let the sun warm me. Before I knew it, my eyes closed, and it seemed as if I were dreaming.

A beautiful woman in a long blue dress was standing and looking at me. "It is horrible in there, is it not?" she asked. "Akin to being in a cage." She spread her arms wide. "How much more glorious are the fresh air and open spaces!"

"Rose?" I wasn't at all surprised. "I should have known I wouldn't find you inside."

"It was a place of torment." Her eyes darkened. "He was an evil man, full of poison and hatred, preaching about God while in league with the devil! He could not abide his son loving me. Do you know why?"

I shook my head.

"He desired me for himself. Oh yes! He told me. He asked me to give up Thomas and wed him instead. When I refused, my fate was sealed. Only I did not have that knowledge then."

"Yet you married Thomas. Why did Amos give his permission?"

"He wished to keep me close." Her face hardened. "Thence he could watch me, touch me, force me into corners and stroke my hair. Vile man! I could not wait to have my own house and escape him. When our home was complete, what a happy day it was. Thomas and I enjoyed our peace, away from them all. Alas, we did not have long." She sighed. "Thomas was a dear man but not a strong one. He was taken only a year after we wed."

"And then you fell in love with Jacob?" I supplied.

Her eyes sparkled. "Indeed I did. And how wonderful it was! His father was enraged of course. He had been pursuing me again, with his youngest barely cold in the ground. But Jacob did not fear him. He saw the truth of things and was strong enough to bear it. They came to blows, and his father disowned him. As if that would have stopped Jacob from wedding me! We were glad to have the old devil out of our lives. We made do, and our precious little black-eyed Susan was born."

"You had a daughter?" I asked in wonder. "She was my...?"

"Many times great-grandmother." Rose smiled. "As am I. That must seem passing strange to you, little one, for here I am your very age! But you are a child to me. How much you resemble my Susan! You have her beautiful face, her dark eyes and hair. You even have the same name. For Susan, in Hebrew, means Lily."

I could see a vision of Rose holding the baby to her breast and singing softly. Then it disappeared, and I heard the sounds of the others returning. I opened my eyes.

"How are you feeling?" Cal asked, sitting down on the rock beside me.

I was still too touched to talk about my experience. "I'm all right. Did anything happen in the house?"

"No, not specifically," Amy said, "but none of us could stay. It was—"

"—hard to breathe," Derek finished. "There are seriously bad vibrations in there. We asked the guide what she knows."

"She told us about Amos and his sons," Cal continued, "and repeated a lot of what Jo learned about Rose. She said Rose died in a fire and that there were rumors about her being a witch. But get this... Rose had a child!"

He looked so excited at producing the information that I felt guilty saying, "I know. She was a little girl with black eyes and hair, and her name was Susan."

Everyone stared at me. "How did you know?" Cal asked.

"I was talking to Rose just before you came. She was standing right there. She showed me the baby."

A buzz broke out as they all asked me questions. At last Cal said, "No wonder the atmosphere in that house is so poisonous. Amos Woodbine was some piece of work."

"He sure was," I replied. "Frustrated passion is a dangerous thing, especially in a man used to getting whatever he wants. Did the guide tell you what happened to Susan?"

"She was out with her aunt when the fire struck Rose's house. Apparently, after Jacob died, the aunt took her to England to be raised.

By then, Amos was gravely ill. He only survived his son by a month. Susan later married a man named Whitehall and then was lost to history."

"There are Whitehalls in my family tree!" I exclaimed. "My aunt had it traced back to the eighteenth century. That proves it!"

"So that's why only you can find the book," Cal said. "Which reminds me, we'd better get walking."

Full of our new information, we set off across the lawn. I went east with Cal. Derek, Jo and Amy went west.

While we hiked, it was Cal's turn to wax poetic about Katy. I chuckled at the end of his catalog of virtues. "Whoever that is, she sounds wonderful," I joked. "You'll have to introduce us sometime."

He looked sheepish. "Well, maybe 'brighter than a supernova' sounds a little over the top, but I swear I expect to see sparks come flying off her at any moment."

"She's a very special person. No one could ask for a better friend." My attention was diverted by the sight of a wooden fence in the near distance. "Do you think we've come to the cemetery?"

A few more strides proved my guess to be correct. There was a historical marker at the gate: *Burying Ground for the Towne of Woodville, established 1680*. "Oh, I love cemeteries."

"You do?"

"Sure. The stones and the statuary tell you a lot about a place's history. And the inscriptions are fascinating. Besides, they're so…peaceful."

"I should hope so!"

We went inside and looked around. The graves were marked mostly by brown sandstone slabs with winged skulls carved on them. "Where are the angels?" Cal asked.

"This was a fire-and-brimstone time. Not everyone could get into Heaven. Cherubs came later, with a more optimistic viewpoint. It's very unusual for a cemetery this old to have survived, but after the smallpox epidemic, the community dwindled, and then William Lychworth purchased the land and kept it a wilderness. Sandstone weathers very well, whereas marble erodes quickly. Half the inscriptions from the early 1800s at Hope are illegible. This place is a real treasure."

"You hang around in Hope Cemetery too?"

"It's a beautiful park. I always walked there from the university."

"While studying the tombs of ancient Egypt? I'm beginning to wonder about you, Lily."

"I do spend a lot of time with the dead, don't I? Maybe I should get help for that," I said dryly.

"Where's Amos?"

"Just look for the showiest memorial. They were status symbols. I'm sure he did himself proud."

It didn't take long to find. We stood together and gazed at the largest and most intricately carved stone. Under the traditional Biblical verses were the words: *Here Lieth the Body of Amos Woodbine, Founder of Our Towne, Most Worthy and Esteemed Citizen. Born in England 1640, died 1693.*

"'Worthy and esteemed'? That's a laugh." Cal shook his head. "The victors really do write history."

Thomas was laid to rest beside his father. "Born in England, 1665, died 1690. So Rose and Jacob must have gotten married in 1691. And she died when she was twenty-four. They only had two years together. Of course there are no graves for them. But who's this?" I bent to look more closely at the stone next to Thomas. "Irene Woodbine. She died in 1689. So she was spared knowing what happened to her family. I guess that was a blessing. I hope you rest in peace, Irene."

Cal checked his watch. "Well, we could probably stay here all day, but we should get moving. We still have some time to search."

But when we met back at the house an hour later, we'd made no progress. We saw no oak trees or boulders, nor did we get any sense that we were going in the right direction. Reluctantly, we had to call it a day. It was beginning to get dark, and we were all tired.

"We'll just have to try again later," Cal said. "You can't expect these things to be easy."

As we drove home, there was a lot of discussion about what we'd learned, but I was mostly silent. I couldn't stop thinking about Rose and the baby she'd held, her precious little black-eyed Susan. *She must have wondered about her mother. What was she told? Rose said their knowledge was passed down from mother to daughter, so she must have been raised by a maternal aunt. I hope Susan was happy.* It was so strange, being faced with relatives I'd never known I had, and it made me more determined than ever to help.

Chapter Twelve

The next morning I slept in very late. I was reading the Sunday newspaper when the telephone rang. I let the answering machine pick up so I could keep eating my cereal. I almost choked at the sound of the caller's voice.

"Lily, it's Yvette. I need to see you. Meet me at the park in back of the conservatory at two o'clock. It's *very* important."

I listened in disbelief. No *"hi,"* no *"please"* and no *"can you...?"* It was just a command. *Who does she think she is?*

I got up and looked at the caller ID. *Private number? What a surprise.* She hadn't left a way to get in touch and refuse her order. She just assumed I would obey.

My first instinct was to ditch her. I was irritated by her arrogance and pretty sure what she wanted to discuss. She would be critical of both Katy and me, and I wasn't going to put up with that.

But as the morning wore away, curiosity began to get the better of me. I didn't have any special plans. I decided I might as well meet her and get it over with. It seemed some kind of showdown was inevitable.

So one thirty found me at the conservatory. The greenhouses were a gem of the park system, five sections devoted to different kinds of flora. The entry hall was filled with seasonal flowers. At that time of year, there were several colors of mums and asters. They led to a model of an old-fashioned front porch with ivy climbing up the wooden façade. The scene was complete with a rocking chair and a birdbath, where two life-like robins perched. I drank in the serenity and then went through a curtain of Spanish moss into the next room, a simulation of a tropical rain forest.

Vivid orchids bloomed behind the thin curtain of water trickling down a rock face. Palm, banana and fig trees grew so tall that they pushed through the glass panels of the roof.

A stream gurgled by, and turtles congregated on the rocks. I loved turtles and stood on a little footbridge watching them. Two were mesmerized by the reflection of sunlight on stone, their necks stretched out as they stared intently. Others were huddled together. A baby was climbing laboriously over the larger shell of an adult.

I was sorry there hadn't been enough time to bring Kent here. *He would have enjoyed this place. If only we could be standing amidst all this beauty together.* I took a penny out of my purse and tossed it into a small pool further on. There was no need to consider what wish to make. It was always the same.

I glanced at my watch. It was 1:50. I made my way into the cactus room. There, the model was of a Spanish mission, and it really did give a feeling of being in the American West. I gazed at prickly pear, pincushion, hedgehog and old-man cacti, the latter covered in long white hairs, trying to fortify myself with the wonder of nature before being confronted with the reality of Yvette. But it was time to leave the conservatory and face her.

She was draped on a bench out back, looking like a model getting ready for a shoot. Her cashmere sweater, designer jeans and suede boots probably cost more than my entire wardrobe. She greeted me without preamble. "Lily. Join me."

Should I curtsey and say, "Yes, Your Majesty"? Yvette didn't seem the type to be affected by sarcasm, so I sat down beside her.

She turned and looked me right in the eye. "I want to talk to you about Cal."

"I didn't expect a friendly chat. Go on."

"He gives the impression of being totally in control. It makes people think they can lean on him. I'm here to tell you he isn't Atlas, and you can't put all your weight on his shoulders."

"I've done no such thing. Cal offered to help me after he read my fortune. *He* initiated it. I didn't even want this Pandora's box to be opened again."

"Interesting you should say that. Who was punished when that box was opened? Not Pandora. Oh sure, she felt bad, but Zeus didn't hold it against her because she couldn't help it. It was the way she was made. No, it was the rest of mankind who suffered from all the evil that was released by her curiosity. Cal has been different since he met you. I don't like it."

"What a surprise." I was angry now. "We're not in nursery school where someone just stole your favorite toy. Cal is his own man, and he doesn't need your permission to do anything."

"How much do you know about his childhood?"

I was thrown off by the sudden change in the conversation. It took me a moment to realize that the answer was, *"Not enough."* Even Katy hadn't mentioned it. "Well," I offered feebly, "I know his mom loves her Welsh heritage and taught him all about it, and his dad's a big jazz fan, which is why he's named Caliman."

"Bravo!" Yvette mocked. "That's all the trouble you've taken to find out, yet he could probably recite your entire biography."

I felt a pang of guilt, remembering the day I'd sensed that Cal was on the brink of a confidence, but then my defenses went up. "I'm not a mind-reader. He has that advantage and the experience to handle it. He's my guide. That seems to be what he wants to concentrate on, not himself. I'd listen if he needed me to."

"Of course you would, but let me enlighten you for now."

A huge crow swept down from the sky with a *screech*. I shrank back involuntarily as it landed right at our feet.

Yvette went on speaking as if it weren't even there. "Cal's parents got divorced when he was ten. It's a miracle they lasted that long. His father was a math professor. Mommy was an anthropologist, specializing in folklore. It was a terrible mismatch, like Cal and your flighty little friend."

"Katy is a very intelligent and good person," I interjected vehemently. "Don't insult her!"

"Oh dear, I'm so sorry. The *last* thing I want is to hurt anybody's feelings." Yvette rolled her perfectly made-up eyes. "Allow me to continue. Mr. Jones already had a girlfriend waiting in the wings, so when Cal visited on weekends, he got locked in his room quite a bit. Dear old Dad was kind enough to provide him with great reading material—science journals and math books. Cal was a gifted student, and he wanted to please the old man, so he learned."

She shifted her position on the bench, and the crow ruffled its feathers. *Why on Earth isn't it flying away?*

"Mrs. Jones also found a new love—the bottle. She drank every night. And the more she drank, the more she became obsessed with her Celtic blood. She stuffed Cal's head full of myths and legends and stories about his supposed druid ancestors. She was thrilled when he developed his 'second sight.' I guess she thought she had another Merlin on her hands. She actually wanted him to go to Stonehenge at the summer solstice and take part in all that neo-pagan nonsense."

The crow squawked as if to punctuate her scorn.

"It was hard for him to shuffle between two such different worlds, trying to make both his parents happy. Thankfully he escaped them when he chose to go to Chicago. He loved it there. But he's never gotten over his need to make sense of things, to understand."

"He wants to find order in chaos," I said, remembering Cal's words to me.

"Yes. He's driven to absorb all the knowledge he can. Knowledge is power, and power leads to control. There was precious little of that in his earlier life."

"How long have you been in love with him?"

I thought the question might put her off her guard, but apparently nothing could rattle that composure.

"A long time. He doesn't feel the same way, I know. Still, there's a very strong connection between us. We've always been open with each other, until you arrived on the scene. Now he's shutting me out. Why would he do that?"

If it were any other woman, I might've had some sympathy for her, but Yvette seemed more like a spoiled child, upset because for the first time, she hadn't gotten something she wanted. "You need to ask Cal." I stood up, anxious to end the uncomfortable encounter. "I have no kind of hold over him. Who he decides to date is his business. We can't choose for our friends." I pushed an image of Stephen and Jenny out of my mind.

Yvette's voice grew sharper. "Is that what you think this is about?"

The crow beat its wings as if agitated by her tone. To my utter astonishment, she reached down and patted it on the head. The bird quieted and stared at me with its black eyes. There was a remarkable intelligence in them.

Yvette straightened. "You don't understand. There's something going on here. Whatever you've let out of that box, Pandora, if Cal gets hurt, you'll have me to reckon with."

I gave her a defiant look and turned away. "Don't bother me again," I said over my shoulder.

I had to force myself to walk slowly back around the building, more shaken than I wanted to admit. I half-expected to feel either Yvette's or the crow's claws suddenly digging into my back. I hadn't considered just how jealous she might be or what sort of paranormal beliefs she practiced. Now I wished I'd gotten up earlier and gone to watch Derek in the dress rehearsal of *The Tempest*. Katy, Cal, Jo and Amy were all there.

It certainly would've been more fun than that meeting with Lady Macbeth.

Thinking of the Bard, I got back in the car and drove over to Hope Cemetery. As I made my way along a path, I could hear bells ringing the hour from the university and the sounds of cheers and whistles from a football game. Two joggers and a teenaged couple passed by me. Squirrels ran to and fro, busily gathering acorns. I felt the familiar calm descend as I walked.

I headed for one of my favorite spots, where three trees stood together. Each was a different color, and the contrast between them was breathtaking. They were very old, with massive knotted trunks and a myriad of heavy branches. The leaves were scarlet, yellow and an orangey gold. They were placed beside a small mausoleum whose shining whiteness accented their beauty even more.

Some of these structures were like grim granite fortresses, but this one reminded me of a real house. The family was all together in there, with an inscription over the door that read: *Blessed be the ties that bind.* I remembered that hopeful hymn from my childhood. It was a peaceful site, if a quirky one.

I knew all the names by heart, for the family clearly had a bent for Shakespeare. I fancied that when the parents, Benedick and Beatrice, had met, they must have taken it for a sign. Their children were christened Edgar, Diana, Frederick and Oliver. The tradition continued into the next generation: Edmund, Malcolm, Rosalind, Bianca, Orlando, Celia and Valentine. At the base was a quote from *As You Like It:*
Now go we in content
to liberty and not to banishment.

I was so used to seeing the words that it took a moment for my brain to catch up to my eyes. I stared in disbelief at the marble as I realized that what I'd just read was an entirely different passage. I scanned it again:
If of life you keep a care,
shake off slumber, and beware:
Awake, awake!

I blinked twice, but the message was still there.

Why would someone alter the tomb after so many years, and with such a different sentiment? I couldn't understand it. *Unless…*

A man with a dog was approaching along the path.

"Hi," I said, stopping him. "I was wondering if you could help me. I forgot my glasses today, and I can't quite read what this says." I pointed at the inscription.

He walked over and peered at it while I patted his golden retriever on the head. "'Now go we in content to liberty and not to banishment.' That's pretty. Is it from the Bible?"

"Shakespeare," I replied distantly. "Thanks very much."

"You're welcome." He moved away, but I stood there for quite some time. Of course the man was correct. The quote now read exactly as it always had. The change had been in my mind. It was a warning from Rose—a warning about Yvette.

She clearly considered me public enemy number one, and I didn't doubt she was capable of carrying out a reckoning. *But will she find a good enough reason? And what means might she use to do it?*

Chapter Thirteen

"Personally, I think Yvette is a witch herself, in both senses of the word." It was the following afternoon, and I'd just told Katy about the park and the strange event in the cemetery. "She just showed up at the end of Derek's rehearsal and invited herself along to the party! I got an upset stomach and had to leave early. It *could* have been something I ate, but I wouldn't be surprised if she's got a voodoo doll with my name on it."

"I think you're safe. It's not as if you stole Cal away from her. They've never dated. I, on the other hand, appear to be a direct threat to him. Why would Rose warn me if Yvette weren't dangerous?"

"She wants to make sure you keep an eye on her. I'd let it be known that you had that meeting. Tell Cal. You don't have to make it dramatic. Just say how lucky he is to have a friend who worries about him so much that she's willing to do anything to keep him out of harm's way."

"Oh, that's perfect. Or I could write a sealed letter and put it in a bank vault with his name on it, to be opened in the event of my death."

Katy shook her head. "That's so cliché. No, don't you kick my ankle! I'm sorry. But I'm serious. Mention it to him without coming down too hard on Yvette, because he's very loyal. I'll do the same thing. And when I meet Cal at his office—and she is always close by—I'll work in a remark about how *you* have protective friends, ghosts helping you, and a cat that can catch crows right out of the sky."

I laughed. "All right. I don't see any reason why I can't bring her up to him. Finding the book is so important. I can't imagine that Cal or Rose would let anything go wrong."

"Speaking of the book, I can help you hunt for it. Cal and I can search the woods, away from everyone else—"

"And I'm sure you'd cover a lot of ground," I said dryly, "but we need a bit more than that. It's like looking for a needle in a haystack."

"Why doesn't Rose just show you where it is? I don't get it. She appears to you, so she should say, 'Ten miles that way, and I'll wait and mark the spot.' Why doesn't she?"

"I don't know. Maybe she doesn't have enough energy for that, or maybe she only wants me alone."

Katy thought about that. "Well, what do you suppose is in it anyway? How to use flowers and plants as medicine? That's what it sounds like. The modern world has lost a lot of valuable information. After we're finished cutting down the rainforests, we'll have destroyed a lot more. Do you really think there's something that can help your mom?"

"I don't know, but I hope so." I'd been wondering about the contents of the book as well. "If keeping it hidden was so important, there must be powerful information in there. After all, Rose said to show it to the 'seeker of knowledge.' Cal's not a doctor though. He's a physicist. What does she know that would interest him?"

"Maybe she was talking about Stephen," Katy suggested.

"No, I don't think so. Cal is the one in this with us. He seems very attuned to Rose. And I can't help but wonder—if she really was a witch—what she might have written in the book. How many secrets did she have in her power?"

"What, you mean like spells? Eye of newt and tongue of frog? I can't see Cal stirring up any cauldrons. Now, if Rose had a grasp of atoms or time and space and could see back to the big bang—"

"Well she's already crossed time and space, hasn't she?" I pointed out. "And she knows spells, because she put some on the book to protect it. We really don't know what's in it, do we?"

Katy looked at me, surprised. "You don't think it's anything dangerous, do you?"

For a moment that thought crossed my mind, but then I shook my head. "No. Rose was a victim, like many other women. It probably is just plant and herb lore. It wouldn't be at all unusual if spells were a part of it. Magic and medicine were indistinguishable for a long time and still are in some cultures. But any knowledge can be dangerous in the wrong hands. That's why she trusts me to find the book and Cal to read it too."

"Right," Katy agreed. "So when are you going to look for it again?"

The answer to that question came the next day. Cal telephoned me at ten in the morning. "Lily, I hope you have tomorrow free. I don't have to work, so I thought maybe we could go back to the park."

"Just the two of us? There's so much ground to cover."

"It can't hurt to give it a try. Besides, you're the key here. If Rose is going to appear, it'll be to you. I'm certain she'll show you the way sooner or later. I think she's just gathering strength."

"Well, I don't really have anything to do that I can't put off. But, Cal..." I hesitated, remembering Yvette's comments. "I hope you don't feel too much pressure."

"What do you mean?" He asked, sounding genuinely surprised.

"You started all this because of me. It's not your responsibility to solve everything. We can wait until we have more help or slow down the pace. I wouldn't mind."

"You're not having second thoughts, are you, Lily? Has something happened?"

"No. I just want to be sure I'm not taking advantage of you. Carolyn said you come to the gallery a lot. You've spent so much time with me. I know you have your own important work to do."

"You're sweet, but I've got no problem at all. As long as you're okay, don't worry about me."

I relaxed. "In that case, tomorrow will be fine."

"Great. I'll buy you lunch at the Glen Orchid Inn. No picnic this time."

The Glen Orchid was an upscale restaurant right in front of a beautiful waterfall. "Deal," I agreed. "What time do you want to leave?"

"Eleven?" Cal suggested.

"That's fine. I'll see you then."

I hung up the phone and went to open a window. The autumn day was another warm one. I was delighted to hear my mockingbird singing. He lived in the trees in my back yard, and I hated to see him go in the fall. He had stayed to grace the last of the good weather. I sat down just to listen for a while.

They really are fascinating creatures. Not only can they imitate other birds but sometimes the objects around them. I had read that in the city they can sound like jackhammers and car horns. Luckily, all the notes my mockingbird hit were sweet. On that day, he was particularly enthralling, and I closed my eyes to enjoy him. When I opened them again, I was standing in the woods, and Rose was there with me. At her side, the big gray wolf sat like an obedient dog.

She smiled. "A lovely song, is it not?"

The mockingbird was still twittering, but nothing else was the same. This time, Rose hadn't come to visit me; I had gone to her.

I stepped back a little nervously. Not only the change but also the power of the woman herself intimidated me.

She saw this and laughed. "You have nothing to fear from me or from this place. It is neither mine nor yours. It is an in-between time, where everything is safe." She gave me a searching look. "It seems a burden to you, the special talents we share. This is because there has been no one to instruct you, no one to help you understand your gifts."

The wolf stirred, and she ruffled its fur.

"But now you have found friends. You will grow in strength and do great things. I will teach you all I know. You can become who you were truly meant to be." She spread out her hands. "Alas, ignorance and superstition still exist. You will not be free of them either, but you can hold up your head and be proud. No harm will come to you. It is time. Tomorrow I will send you a sign, one that you cannot mistake. You will find the book, Lily, and all will be well. Go now."

The song of the mockingbird was still in my ears, but suddenly I was back in my own house, and the music was outside my own window. I felt as though I had awakened from a dream.

Cleo was rubbing around my legs as if she were alarmed.

"It's all right, gumdrop," I said, picking her up. "We're going to have to get used to these things, it seems."

I sat for a while stroking her, lost in thought. It was a knock on the front door that brought me out of my reverie. Putting Cleo on the floor, I went to answer it. It was only the man coming to read the water meter. In spite of visions and books and special gifts, life went on.

So does housework, I reminded myself. I got out the vacuum cleaner, and Cleo ran to hide under the bed until the monster was gone. It felt good to be doing something so normal. I actually enjoyed dusting and scrubbing and washing my clothes. My everyday life was like an anchor, one I suspected I was going to rely on more and more.

That night there was a terrific thunderstorm. The constant lightning and the sound of the thunder and wind made my sleep a restless one. I had strange, disjointed dreams. Rose was writing in the book, with blood instead of ink. Kent and I were flying in a small plane that suddenly plummeted down towards the ground below. I screamed and hid myself in his arms, but instead of comforting me he said sternly, "Don't lose control."

The scene shifted to a Halloween party, where I was dressed in a pink tutu and everyone wore masks. I thought I was dancing with Kent, Stephen and Cal, but no one spoke, and I couldn't see through their disguises with any certainty. I was spun around in circles until I was dizzy and had to sit down. Two dark-haired women were in chairs next to me.

"Don't worry," one said. "You'll soon feel better."

The other shook her head sadly. "Don't listen to her. You mustn't believe a word she says."

Then ghosts took over the floor. They moved back and forth in a stately waltz. All the guests applauded except for me. I was staring at Cleocatra, who came into the room and jumped up on the table. "Be careful," she said. "Beware of the wolf." And a large gray wolf with glowing red eyes barged into the crowd, howling and knocking down everything in its path.

The jack-o-lanterns fell, their candles igniting the tablecloths, the curtains and people's clothes. Soon there was a raging inferno. I could feel the flames coming closer and their heat blooming on my face. With a gasp of terror, I woke myself up.

Cleocatra was lying across my chest, and the room was bright with lightning. I lay there trembling and took a long time to go back to sleep. Once I finally dozed off again, it was only two hours until bright sun and Cleo were waking me again.

The effect of the nightmares stayed with me until after I'd eaten breakfast, showered and dressed. By then I felt better and I told myself, *It's only because today is so important.* I knew we were going to find the book and put Rose's spirit to rest. Still, I jumped when the doorbell rang. Even though I was expecting Cal, for a moment I was frightened. *Don't be silly*, I told myself and let him in.

"That was some storm last night. Did it keep you awake too?"

"I covered up the circles under my eyes," I joked. "Do I still look that awful?"

"Of course you don't. You are your usual lovely self. I just wondered because I feel like I hardly slept at all. Besides the racket, I was nervous about today. I feel like we're getting very close. It's a big responsibility."

"Me too." I was relieved that he understood. "I think we should call everyone and have them meet us tonight. It's best to share something as important as the book. We don't even really know what's going to be in it."

"You're right. Just like they say, a little knowledge is a dangerous thing. We want to have everyone present to help Rose, in case she needs us."

"Everyone?" It was the opening I'd been waiting for. "Do you think Yvette will come? She doesn't seem to like me, and honestly, it makes me uncomfortable."

"Oh, don't worry about her. That's just the way she is. It takes her a long time to warm up to people. But she has a very good heart once you get past her armor. She wants to help."

I didn't believe him, but I said, "Good, because we *are* getting close." I told him about the vision of Rose I'd had while listening to the mockingbird.

Cal was thrilled. "She definitely said today? Lily, that's wonderful!"

Cleo came into the room and hissed at Cal.

"Now that's not nice," I chided her, bending down to scratch behind her ears. "I'm sorry I have to leave you all day, but you'll be fine." I straightened up and grabbed my purse from the coffee table. "Let's go."

In silent agreement, perhaps because we were nervous, we didn't mention Rose in the car. Cal talked about physics, and I held forth on ancient Egypt.

I told him about one of my favorite myths, *The Days Upon the Year.* "The sky goddess Nut was pregnant, and Ra, the supreme solar deity, was afraid of more gods and goddesses coming along and threatening his power. So he put a curse on Nut, saying she could not give birth on any day of the year. The Egyptian year had 360 days at the time, but Thoth, the lunar deity, played a board game with the moon and won extra light, enough for five days."

"There's a full moon tonight," Cal remarked.

"Yes, and it should be gorgeous. I'm glad the sky is clear."

"So Nut had her children?"

"Yes, one on each of the days—Osiris, Isis, Seth, Nephthys and Horus the Elder. That made the Egyptians the first to have a calendar of 365 days. But it was considered very bad luck to do anything important on The Days Upon the Year. They added them onto the end after the late harvest, and they weren't part of any month. They were too dangerous. They called them The Days of the Demons."

"They certainly had a way with words. Look, Lily! A fox!"

We'd entered the park, and I turned my head just in time to see the elusive creature dart into the trees. "Wow. That's unusual. I've only seen a fox once in here before."

"It's a good omen," Cal proclaimed. "It's hard to wait. I want to go find that book *now*."

"Forget it. You promised me lunch, and we're going to have it."

"Of course. After all, we'll need strength for the task ahead. Now where's the turn for this restaurant?"

I directed him up a long, winding road to where the Glen Orchid stood at the top of a hill. It was a beautiful house from the mid-1800s, converted into an inn and restaurant. In back of it were the Middle Falls, one of three stunning cascades in the park. Cal and I stood by the stone wall and watched for a few minutes as the water pounded down. It was an awesome sight. The mist blew into our faces, and a rainbow shimmered overhead. It was hard to tear myself away, but I was hungry.

We walked across the terrace and around to the main door. A long, carpeted hallway led us into the dining room. We got a table next to the window, where we could see a flower garden still in bloom. To my delight, a chipmunk was sitting in it, gnawing an acorn. The atmosphere was relaxed and soothing.

I ordered my seasonal favorites, squash soup and a turkey and brie sandwich. There was even pumpkin cheesecake for dessert, but I had to get it to go.

Cal ate sparingly in spite of the wonderful food. I knew he was anxious to get on the trail. As soon as my Styrofoam container came, he stood up and pushed back his chair. "Well, this has been great, but duty calls. Are you ready for the hunt, Lily?"

"Ready as I'll ever be." I got up from the table as well, making sure to take my cheesecake. I couldn't resist a last lingering look at the waterfall outside before we went back to the car.

We drove past the old house we had visited the other day and stopped at the place where I'd had my vision of Rose.

"We may as well wait here," Cal said, "since we don't know where we're going."

"She said she would send a sign that I won't mistake. Let's just sit here a while until—"

The words died on my lips as the unmistakable sign appeared. From out of nowhere, a gray wolf padded towards us. He stood looking at us, as if conveying a message. Then he turned and began walking slowly away.

I heard Cal release his indrawn breath. "Come on, Lily!" He started after the animal.

But I noticed that the wolf was moving parallel to the road. "Cal, wait! It could be miles, and we left our equipment in the trunk. Let's follow in the car for as long as we can."

Cal returned reluctantly. The wolf waited while we climbed back into the car, then loped off once more. We set off after him, driving to our date with destiny.

Chapter Fourteen

After a minute of swerving and drifting between lanes, I told Cal firmly, "You watch the road, and I'll watch the wolf." I kept my eyes glued to the animal, fretting as it wove in and out of the trees. I lost sight of it as we neared the old cemetery, and I leaned my head out the window. *There. Was that movement among the stones?* After a breathless interval, I saw him again, still leading us on. Neither Cal nor I spoke, keeping our eyes on the moving shape.

It seemed no time at all before we arrived at two large boulders in front of an ancient oak tree. Cal parked the car, and the wolf seemed to nod its head and then disappeared into the woods.

We sat for a few minutes, almost afraid to get out. "This is the place," I whispered. "It's just like in my dream. We're behind where Rose and Jacob's house used to be."

Cal stared at the land without saying anything, as still as a statue.

I finally had to tap him on the shoulder. "Are you okay?"

He turned his face towards me as if I had awakened him from a deep sleep. "What?" he asked in confusion.

"Should we get started?"

"Oh, yes." He rubbed his eyes. "Sorry. I had a funny feeling there."

"I understand. I don't do this kind of thing every day either."

"We're actually about to find it, aren't we?"

"I think so." All my senses were heightened, and goose bumps prickled my skin. For Cal, the book was an academic treasure that would vindicate Rose. I had an even stronger, more personal desire for her to be at rest, but I'd also be bringing a long-lost family history back to light. And maybe—just maybe—I'd be able to help my mom become whole again.

Cal and I looked at each other and moved in unspoken assent. He collected the shovels and spades from the trunk of the car. I took a scrunchie from my purse and twisted my hair up into a ponytail. Abandoning the dressy sweater I'd worn over my shirt for the restaurant, I rolled up my pant legs, switched my flat shoes for sneakers and put on a pair of gardening gloves.

"We may as well start here." Cal indicated the spot where the wolf had stopped.

I pushed my shovel in, balancing on the edges the way I had when I was a child.

I almost fell over when Cal's voice suddenly rang out. "'Graves at my command...Have waked their sleepers, oped, and let 'em forth...By my so potent art.'"

I looked at him in astonishment. "What?"

He stared back at me. "I don't know why I said that. I remembered it from *The Tempest*. I think I know that play as well as Derek by now."

"Cheerful thought to start on. Zombies! Thanks."

"Sorry. I've gone a little loopy. Don't mind me. Just dig!"

The ground was soft from the nighttime rainfall, and at first we made good progress, but the deeper we went, the harder it got. My back hurt more and more, and my breaks lasted longer and longer. I marveled at Cal's stamina. While I sat in the car drinking water, he barely paused. "You're working like a man possessed. Why don't you rest for a while?"

"I'm fine." He wiped a sleeve across his face. "Three hundred years is a long way down, and we have to find it before sunset."

"We should've asked the others for help." I sighed.

"No. This is meant for you and me to discover. I can feel it. We're getting close."

A cloud passed across the sun. I glanced up in surprise, because the sky had been crystal clear all day. At the same time, Cal drove the shovel in once more, and we both heard a metallic *clang*.

Cal froze, and a tremor went through my body. Very slowly, I took a spade and knelt. The dirt fell away as if the box beneath it wanted to be free. I was aware of Cal dropping down beside me.

"At last," he breathed. He reached to grasp the ring on the coffer lid, but the moment he touched it, he gave a howl of pain.

"What is it? What's wrong?" I cried.

"It burned me!" Cal's hand was shaking. "Fool! I should have known. You must be the one to take it, Lily."

Bewildered, I stretched out my fingers and touched the surface quickly. *Nothing.* I held my hand there longer and felt only coolness. "It's all right," I said. "It doesn't hurt. Try again."

Cal did, cautiously. There was no shock this time. "You have identified yourself," he said with satisfaction. Together, we pulled the box from the ground.

He nodded. My heart pounding, I flipped back the catch. It moved easily, not as if it had been closed for over 300 years.

The first thing I saw was a piece of black velvet cloth, perfectly preserved. "She really did protect it," I said with awe. Taking it up carefully, I unwound it from the volume it enrobed. The book was finally there before us.

It was large and leather bound, with symbols covering the front. I opened it gently and read on the inside cover, "'My name is Rose Adams. Herein lies the knowledge gathered from long and arduous study by many generations of my Family.' Oh Cal, there's a list! Her mother, grandmother, all of the maternal relations, for—it must be over 300 years! I can't wait to copy this down!"

I turned to a page of parchment filled with Rose's script. I saw the medicinal uses of honey and drawings of plants used to bring a fever down. Opposite those was a diagram of the night sky labeled: *How to Find Fortunes in the Stars*, and then…*Poisons: Doses for Sickness, Doses for Death.*

I gasped out loud and closed my eyes. Images were searing themselves into my brain, terrible things I didn't want to see. There was Rose concocting a potion and giving it to Thomas. There were spells for inflicting illness and torment, for calling up spirits and summoning familiars. I felt as if I were going to be sick. "Cal!" I choked. "It's all been a lie! She's evil. Rose is evil! She was a black witch, and she killed her husband so she could be with Jacob!"

"That's not fair, Lily," I heard Cal say. It was hard to concentrate on his voice, and I couldn't resist when he took the book from my hands. "She had to defend herself. You have no idea what it was like for her, with enemies all around. She could heal as well as hurt. She came so close to the line between life and death. The knowledge in here is priceless. It will enable me to look into the heart of the universe! I can bring her back!"

Bring her back? My eyes opened painfully. Cal still sat beside me, yet it was not Cal. Chills ran up and down my spine. I tried to keep my voice steady.

"Cal, get a hold of yourself. Remember who you are. Caliman Jones, physicist. You work at the university, and you're dating Katy Morrison, and you lead a group of psychics and help them protect themselves. Remember the light? Think of it surrounding you—"

He laughed, a horrible sound that made me quiver. "Stop your babbling. What do I care for any light? I know who I am, and I know what I can do. We are grateful that you have obtained the book for us." He replaced it reverently in the box. "Now come along." He grasped my arm and pulled me up. "We have work to do."

"I'm not going to help you!" I cried, struggling to get free of him, but his grip was like iron.

"You will," he said. "You must. You are of the blood. You alone can right the wrongs they did to us. The savages burned my Rose alive! They called my death an 'accident' as they shot the gun four times. Now, at last, we shall be free again. Death cannot part us. Nothing can!"

"Jacob?"

Both Cal and I turned at the voice.

"Let her go, my love. I know how long you have waited, but there is no need for force. Lily is family. She will realize the course she must take."

Rose was standing beside us. Her long, dark hair was free, tumbling over the shoulders of her golden gown. She walked up to Caliman and took his face in her hands. Then she kissed him and sighed. "Soon, sweetheart. We have borne the waiting thus far. In but a little while, our bodies shall be joined once more." She gave her attention to me. "Lily, you should not be frightened. I will never harm you. You are my flesh and blood. This book is your heritage."

"I want no part of it!" I shouted. "It's evil!"

"That is not so. It is knowledge, and I labored long to gain it. My mother began my teaching, but I soon surpassed her skills. I absorbed all the readings, the recipes and spells. I practiced until I was able to create my own. When my young sister fell ill, it was I who saved her. It was I who counseled the women of the town who came to me for help. What they did with the information I gave them was their concern. It never weighed upon my conscience."

I imagined what that "information" might have consisted of. "And now you expect to come back and start all over again? How could you!"

Rose looked mystified. "How could I desire to live? Long to be reunited with the man I love? What would you have me do? Forsake Jacob and condemn us both to eternal darkness?"

"You murdered Thomas!"

"He was sickly and cared no more for life. Why should his death have been prolonged? He asked me to release him. It was an easy passing, and he went to join his God. I was free then to have the husband I deserved, one who shared my passion and could return it. I wanted a child, a family. It is my right to take back that which was denied me."

"It's *not* your right to hurt other people!" I looked in despair at Cal, who was watching us intently. "How did he ever threaten you? What are you doing to his mind?"

"I need him." Rose glanced over. "Jacob does not have my abilities. His spirit must have a home until his physical body is formed. Your friend is the perfect host. Such brilliance! And so much hunger. He wants to understand. He *needs* to understand. I will satisfy that wish, and he will help satisfy mine."

"At what cost?" My voice was shaking. "Cal's life? His soul?"

Rose seemed surprised. "I cannot determine the fate of souls. Only their owners may do that. As for his life, he will not be harmed. His wits will wander of course. The burden of so much knowledge will be too great for them. But before the end, the secrets of creation will be revealed to him. I deem he would consider it a fair exchange."

I winced at the thought of Cal being left an empty husk. "That's not for you to decide. You can't just take people's brains and hearts and play with them like game pieces. No matter how much you suffered, Rose, it doesn't justify destroying innocent victims."

"Do not speak to me of innocence." Rose's beautiful face twisted with malice. "My Susan was only a babe, but the mob of murderers who came to my home would have burned her alive with me! My child was left an orphan, forced to leave everything she knew and loved." Her expression of maternal torment appeared genuine as she went on. "My sister raised her abroad as best she could, but Elizabeth was not well versed in the old ways. Her illness left her weak, and she did not have the book. Little by little, our power began to slip away. With each generation, more was lost. You are the strongest in many, many years." She was almost glowing with triumph now. "Once I can properly instruct you, the glory of our family will shine again. Think upon it, Lily. You shall take your place as the most accomplished scholar and the greatest artist of this day. Your mother, happy and whole, will gladly accept your Englishman. It shall be a marriage of both love and power. In time, the two of you will become parents, and the legacy will continue. Is that not a noble goal? Why should lesser lives interfere with it?"

"Lesser lives?" I repeated. I thought of all the help Cal had given me, the way he had overcome challenges to rise to the top of his field, how much Katy liked him, how he had carved a face from an apple. So many things, both great and small, made us all human. *How dare this witch claim that any life isn't valuable?* I suddenly wished with all my might that I did have some magic, just so I could see her crumble into dust that very minute.

Rose regarded me steadily. "I know your mind, my Lily. You are still young and tender. You believe in a world in which everyone is treated fairly, where it is safe to love and no one will begrudge you your talents. Such a world does not exist." She pointed a finger at me. "Your beauty will bring you heartache. Your skill will call down envy. Your gift will frighten the wary until their whispers grow loud against you. Consider your own situation!"

Her eyes were locked on mine. As much as I wanted to, I couldn't look away. She spoke with such conviction that I found myself actually listening.

"What have you done to deserve your present fate? You had honest employment, but because of another's dishonesty, that is gone. Your beautiful paintings? Yes, you inherited your talent from Jacob. And how many have you attempted lately?" She shook her head. "The joy is gone and with it your ability. You cannot be with the man you love. Your mother's mind is unraveled, and foolish doctors are altering yours with poison. How are you responsible?"

Her voice was hypnotic. How many times I had questioned those very things. *Why should I be so unlucky? It really isn't—*

"Fair?" Rose touched my arm tenderly. "No, it is not. And if you continue this way, it will only worsen. Life is harsh, Lily. You need to defend yourself and strike back against it. You need to make your own future. Jacob and I, we will help you."

"But..." I could feel my resolve weakening. "I don't want to hurt anyone."

"Why should you? It will not be necessary unless you are attacked. Think instead of the good you can do. Protect the ones you love. Make them happy." She could see how much that idea appealed to me, and she stretched out her hands. "Never have a care for money again. Imagine no longer struggling to meet the daily demands of living. You will be free to devote yourself to art and study. With your husband by your side, you may travel anywhere you wish. Yet your fortune shall be your own. You will not be dependent on his."

How easily she seemed to read the secrets of my heart. It did bother me that Kent and I were unequal in that regard. I didn't want him to financially support me. I wanted to make my own name in both art and archaeology.

Rose's sympathetic tone went on like a siren song. "Everything will be as it should be for you. Jacob and I long to be together again, just as you and your Kent do. Why is that wrong?" Her words were pleading. "We were cruelly torn apart and robbed of our lives and our daughter. There was no justice for us. Now we shall have a family again. You know nothing is more important than family. What joy it will be for me to become acquainted with your mother and have the chance to watch your children grow!"

I could almost see myself ensconced in a cozy nursery with Kent, gazing down on our sleeping baby. *We would be good, loving parents, and the scars of our own childhood pain would be erased. Mom and Ursula would be thrilled.* "But what about Cal?" My conscience struggled not to be swept into the whirlpool of this perfect dream. "It isn't right for him to suffer."

"Lily, believe me, the soul will choose that which it truly wants. Your friend desires understanding above all else. That is why I had no difficulty reaching him. His greatest wish is to look into the heart of nature and find order there. And so he shall. If he is not the same afterward, what does it matter? His dream could never have come true but for us."

"It is worth the sacrifice," Cal's voice suddenly said. "It is what the seeker was born for."

I stared hard at him. I remembered Cal telling me that he lived to find the truth. *If he actually discovers it, will that be his ultimate happiness?* "I don't believe in black magic." *Is it really me still talking?* "I won't have any killing or anyone else being possessed."

Rose nodded her head. "That is well, but I cannot promise that I will not take measures if we are ever threatened." Her eyes misted. "I lost my child, and I will never let harm befall one of my own again."

Yes, she was family, and so was Jacob. Without them, I would not have even been alive. *Everything will work out this way.* The thought of being free from worry and pain and fear made me dizzy. I would have slumped to the ground if there hadn't been so many fairy stones there.

"But how will you do it?" I asked. "How will Jacob manifest? He won't need Cal's body?"

"No. I still have my original form, and Jacob shall have his. The book contains the spell to draw his energy back from the void. He and Caliman will accomplish this with our help. Then I shall be made whole in this world again."

"Aren't you now?" She looked very real to me.

"Not completely. I am able to appear before you because of our kinship. I cannot stay for long. But soon I shall be solid again and may embrace you with all the love in my heart. Go with Jacob, Lily. Darkness is approaching, and we must prepare for the moonrise. There are things you need to gather. Do not be afraid. You are so much stronger than you realize. I must rest a while, but I will return for the Summoning to lend my aid."

Her image began to blur around the edges. "Our first act will be to heal your mother, I swear." She walked over to Cal and kissed him again, much more fiercely. "Take care of our Lily, my darling. It is almost over. We shall reclaim the lives that were stolen from us." And right out of Cal's arms, she dissolved into mist.

I tugged at his hand. "Come on! We haven't got much time. What is it we need to find?"

He seemed to be trying to focus. "Plants," he mumbled. "Incense and dirt from the graveyard. It's all written down." He opened the heavy pages of the book and began reading. "I will search for these items. I know they still grow here." It was surreal to hear Cal speaking words that were really Jacob's. I wondered what part of his consciousness was left inside.

"All right. Then I'll get the dirt. Does it have to be from-from a grave?" My hands were trembling. I hated the thought of what lay ahead, but it had to be done.

"It must be unconsecrated, no hallowed ground. Dig on the edges, where the suicides and lost souls were allowed to lie." An expression of anger and disgust crossed his face. "Were they not gracious in their charity? A handful of soil will suffice." He handed me the shovel. "Fill this and bring it back so we may store it."

I nodded, took the tool, and swung it at his head.

Chapter Fifteen

To my amazement, he actually fell down. In spite of my fear and determination, I didn't know I had it in me to deliver such a blow. I could have sworn I'd missed him, but there he was, lying on the ground, stunned. I knew I had to keep moving before I could ponder what I'd just done. I reached into his pocket and felt for the car keys, my eyes glued to his face. There was no reaction. *I'm sorry, Cal. It's for your own good.* My fingers found the keychain and grasped it. Then I picked up the book, feeling like I was holding a ticking bomb, and shoved it back into the box. I had to destroy it, but first I had to get away.

I ran to the car and slid behind the wheel. Scenes from a dozen horror movies went through my mind as I turned the ignition. *What if it doesn't start and I suddenly see Cal, Rose and the wolf pressing up against the windows?* Breathing a prayer of thanks when the engine kicked over, I drove off with the tires squealing. I didn't stop until I was back at the Glen Orchid Inn.

My first instinct was to throw the book into the waterfall. *The hammering force would surely rip it apart.* I was actually at the overlook when I paused to consider, *How can I be sure? What if the thing survives the trip the way barrels sometimes do at Niagara?* Rose had put protective spells on it, after all. I couldn't risk it floating away down the Genesee River to be found by anyone else. Besides, I would need a very strong arm to hit the target, and at least fifteen people crowded around the wall would be reporting me to the authorities.

No, the book will have to be burned. That's the safest bet. I'll take it home, call in reinforcements, and get rid of it.

With that decided, I returned to the main desk inside the inn. I told my altered tale with a barely controlled panic that was all too real. My friend and I had eaten lunch, I explained, gone on a drive through the park and stopped to take a walk. He had begun acting strangely when he saw a fox. "He was bitten by one when he was a child," I heard myself saying. "It had rabies, and he almost didn't survive. He developed post-traumatic stress disorder. Now he's run off, and I'm afraid he might injure himself."

The silver-haired matron who was listening to this farrago of lies was understandably doubtful. I realized too late that I probably should've called from my cell phone after I was well away, but I had to be certain that someone would look for Cal and get him safely to a hospital. I forged ahead before the woman could go and get some security guards.

"He's a physicist who works at the university. His name is Caliman Jones. He's perfectly normal unless something triggers an episode. Then he can get quite…aggressive." *There, that should do it. They won't take a chance on anyone violent roaming around a state park.* "He'll be confused and might not remember who he is. He'll be fine once he gets care."

It was obvious whom the woman really thought needed care. "Let me go and—" she began.

Inspiration suddenly struck. "Wait a moment," I said. "I'll give you the name and number of his doctor." I pulled a piece of paper out of my purse and began writing. "I'll put in Cal's description too. That will make it easier for you, won't it?" *And make me seem more legitimate as well.*

"All right, Miss…?"

"Ashton," I supplied. "Katy Ashton. Oh! I just remembered. His driver's license is in the glove compartment. I'll go get it while you notify the rangers. Be back in a minute."

The woman was already picking up the phone as I turned and forced myself not to run to the parking lot. Once I was out of earshot, I grabbed my cell and called Stephen. "Listen," I said when his answering machine picked up, "a lady from the Glen Orchid Inn—or maybe the police, I'm not sure—will be trying to get a hold of you. I need you to go along and say you're Cal's doctor and that he has PTSD. Fox. Rabies. Okay? I'm leaving now. I should be there in about thirty minutes. Cal's gone crazy, and a real witch is loose. I'll see you soon."

Next I dialed Katy. I had to leave her a message too. "Stay away from Cal!" I warned. "Don't talk to him, listen to him or—above all else—see him. He's changed, Katy…literally. Trust me on this. I'll explain later."

The drive home seemed to take an eternity. I was terrified that Rose would suddenly materialize in the seat next to me or that the wolf would leap out of the darkness and force me off the road. It was hard to concentrate on the steering wheel without looking around.

But it appeared that my timing had been good. I figured Rose had used a lot of energy to manifest for so long in the park and would need to rest up. It was the same for the wolf. And with Cal in a weakened state, hopefully Jacob was out of commission. I could burn the book, and everything would be all right.

But then a new thought began to creep into my mind. *Should I destroy the repository of all that knowledge right away? Or should I have Stephen read through it and see if it contains anything useful? What if there really are lost secrets of healing that can help my mother or anyone else? It is possible. There could be important family information too.*

I mulled this over, weighing the pros and cons. Before I realized it, I was pulling into Stephen's driveway, praying that he would be there.

He was, but when he opened the door to let me in, his face was like a thundercloud. "Lily Evans, where have you been?" he demanded. "I've called your cell at least ten times. Why did you leave me that insane message? I had to tell a park ranger that I am a doctor and that I know Caliman Jones, but I couldn't lie and say he's my patient. Do you know how much trouble I would be in? Why is a search party hunting for him? What in the—"

I interrupted the flow of words with an impatient wave of my hand. "I'm sorry, Stephen, but I couldn't answer the phone while I was driving. I was going way too fast, and I had to stay alert for Rose and the wolf. I'm afraid they'll be turning up soon. Cal and I were at Lychworth, but he's been possessed by Jacob. I got away with the book, so now we have to pick up Katy and get over to my house and grab Cleo."

He stared at me and, when I was finished babbling, steered me inside to the sofa. "Lie down," he ordered, taking the box and setting it on the floor. "I'm going to elevate your legs. It will make you feel better." He placed two cushions under me and took off my shoes. "You're cold. I'll get a blanket. I still have the one your mom made for me, remember?"

I couldn't help but smile in spite of all that was happening. The blanket had been a Christmas gift designed soon after we'd gotten engaged. I never knew how my talented mother had gone so far astray. The decorations were awful. Mom had put in various toys, as if Stephen were five years old: a spinning top, a drum, a sled, a rubber ball, and a jack-in-the-box whose head resembled nothing less than a killer clown. A tree with two huge ornaments took up all the room, along with a pair of children holding hands, a boy in a cowboy outfit and a girl in a tutu. "How could I forget this?" I murmured when it was settled over me. "It's the weirdest gift she ever gave." But it was a comfort nonetheless.

"It's the best gift I ever got. All that time she spent so it would be unique. I love it."

It struck me again that if we had gotten married, my mom really would have been gaining a son.

"Now take some nice, deep breaths. You're safe here. Everything is going to be fine." Stephen opened up his medical bag.

I was jolted out of my brief respite. "No it isn't!" I tried to struggle up and felt nausea sweeping over me. "I don't know if Cal's been caught yet, and with Jacob in control, he's capable of anything. We've got to check on Cleo and hide this box!"

Stephen sat down beside me. "Lily," he said gently, "you're obviously traumatized. You need to rest and—"

I gritted my teeth in frustration. *How can I make him understand what is going on when I've kept it all a secret from him?* "I know it sounds strange," I said as Stephen's raised eyebrow showed quite clearly that he was replacing "strange" with *"crazy"* in his mind. "But Cal is not himself anymore. We went to Lychworth to have lunch, and we—um—dug up this box with a book in it. Cal flipped out."

"Did he hurt you?"

"No, not physically, but he thinks the book will give him special powers, and he wants me to help him use them. He won't stop until he gets it back. He's dangerous!"

"You said you called the police, right?"

"Yes, but Cal's very familiar with the park. He could've hidden or convinced someone to give him a ride. He still has his own intelligence, even if Jacob is directing it now. I need to try Katy again. Hand me my purse."

"*I* will call Katy," Stephen said, "and then the police. *You* will lie quietly until I'm sure you shouldn't be in the hospital."

I knew that tone would brook no argument. I suffered the stethoscope, blood-pressure cuff and penlight shining in my eyes.

"Did you take your meds today?" he asked.

"Not the ones I need now."

"Don't you carry extras?"

"No. I don't usually expect to run across witches and madmen during the day."

"Yeah, about that." Stephen put away his instruments. "Obviously something triggered this, and I'm sure it was very real. But you must recognize that no supernatural beings are involved. Let's deal with the immediate problems." He was in his element now. "We need to keep you safe from Jones and put your mind at rest. I'll get in touch with my friend Jason. He's a policeman. If he's busy, he can find someone else to go to your house. Katy can meet us here, and then we'll leave together. You can take your meds and sleep in your own bed with Cleo, okay?"

I felt terrible, and I had a pounding headache. Rose's main force might have been exhausted for the present by my escape from her old home and Cal's presence as a magnifier, but I could still sense her energy clawing at the edges of my mind. The struggle against her had exhausted me. I wanted nothing so much as a deep, dreamless sleep. "Okay," I agreed, knowing we still had time before Cal could be back in town. "I'm glad the cop is your friend. It might be hard to explain why I hit somebody over the head with a shovel and stole his car."

"You *what?*"

"I told you I had to get away! I'd be in a graveyard summoning the dead right now if I hadn't."

Stephen's face was white, and I was afraid he might fall over.

"Take some deep breaths," I advised, squeezing his hand.

"Lily…" His voice was faint. "Did you actually assault Dr. Jones?"

"Well, sort of. It was more a case of trying to stop Jacob."

"And you stole his car?"

"How else was I going to leave the park? There's no bus service."

Poor Stephen. He looked as if I'd smacked him with a shovel too.

"Don't worry." I tried to reassure him. "Cal isn't dead or anything. I didn't swing that hard. And it was self-defense."

"Against…witchcraft?" Stephen said the word as if it hurt his mouth.

"Yes. Cal…er, Jacob…Jacal grabbed me and was going to force me to take part in a black magic ceremony." I decided that details of my own role were unnecessary. "So I ran. He'll be coming after me because of that." I gestured at the box. "The book inside contains the spell he thinks will bring people back to life."

Stephen's quick medical mind analyzed the crisis. "Then I'll tell Jason that you were threatened first. You were having lunch when Jones suggested going for a walk. You ended up at an old cemetery, and Jones forced you to help him dig for this box. You got a hold of the shovel to defend yourself. There was a struggle, and he was hit. You showed up here dirty and hysterical. Got it?"

I hadn't even remembered that I was grubby from digging. "Oh no. Your sofa! The blanket! I'm sorry." My eyes lit on two half-full wine glasses on the coffee table beside me. It is strange how the mind can be distracted by small details at such a time. "Stephen, did you have a date? Was it with Jenny?"

"Yes and yes. But it's all right. She's used to emergencies. Now listen." He stilled my hand as I plucked at the blanket. "Don't worry. It can be cleaned. What's important to remember is that all of this is Jones's fault. When Jason or any other officer talks to you, that's what you tell them. Can you do it?"

I nodded.

"Okay. Good girl. I'll be back in a minute. Stay there!"

He went into the kitchen, and I could hear the murmur of a conversation. When he returned, he had a glass of water. "Jason is on his way to your place now. He's going to wait until we get there and keep a lookout for Jones, so Cleo has her own personal guard. Now I'll get Katy over here."

He handed me my purse so I could fish out my cell. "She's programmed in," I told him. "First one."

Stephen had no sooner touched the phone than it began to ring. "It's her," he said. "Drink your water."

"Stephen?" Katy's voice was shrill with anxiety. "Is Lily with you?"

"Yes, and we need you here too. Can you come to my house right away?"

"What in the world is happening? She left me the weirdest message. I don't—"

"Katy, please just come. I'll explain everything when we see you."

"And DON'T talk to Cal, no matter what!" I shouted. "Promise!"

"Okay, okay." She sounded scared and exasperated at the same time.

"Thanks." Stephen ended the call. "There now. All taken care of. Soon you'll be safe and sound at home. We just have to wait and see what kind of story Jones turns up with, but at least we got to the police first."

"He's going to be in a lot of trouble. Looting an archaeological site is serious." I started to giggle. "I've finally conducted my first excavation. And it wasn't in Egypt either like I always imagined. It was digging up my own family tree!"

I laughed until Stephen dashed cold water on my face. Suddenly sober, I gazed up at him, blinking.

"I know how much strain you're under honey," he said, "but you're going to get through this. It's not your fault. Whatever Jones did, he'll be held accountable for it. You'll feel better as soon as you take your medicine and get some sleep. Now drink this water. Do you want me to ask Dr. Carson if he can come see you? That might help."

It usually irritated me when he mentioned Dr. Carson, but at that moment, I felt a strange mixture of gratitude and sadness.

"Oh, Stephen, I really wish he *could* help, but there's nothing he can do about this. I know you don't believe in the supernatural, but just look in that box and take out the book. We're up against witchcraft. We really are."

"I think we should ignore it until we can give it to Jason. It's obviously upsetting you."

"Give it to Jason? NO! We can't do that!"

"Of course we can. We have to. It's evidence."

"But…" Conflicting emotions tore at me. I wanted it off my hands, but I felt responsible for it as well. "It's too dangerous to be let out into the world!"

"The police will take care of it, Lily. Don't worry."

"They won't know what to do." In fact, I realized with a jolt, I had no clear idea of how to deal with it either. *Who can I turn to for advice? Are the rest of our group trustworthy, or will they side with Cal?* Of course I had no confidence in Yvette, but I found it hard to credit that the others—especially Derek and Jo—would have any part in such evil. *Should I be warning them too?*

"It'll be locked up and perfectly safe," Stephen was saying. "Then it will go back to whoever claims it, probably the state. It has to have historical value."

I sat bolt upright. "It belongs to *me*!"

Stephen was taken aback by my vehemence. "You, of all people, know that isn't true. Remember Professor Briggs? You exposed him for having stolen artifacts. It's not up to you to decide what happens to that book. Put it out of your mind."

"You don't understand." I clutched at his arm. "It's part of my family heritage. That's the reason only I could find it. Rose, the witch—she wrote it, and she was an ancestor of mine. She and her husband—that's Jacob, the one who's taken over Cal—buried it in their back yard. I didn't know it had black magic in it. She told me there were spells of healing that could help Mom and all humankind." I waved my hand to dismiss any objections. "It has to be destroyed. Of course I recognize that, but maybe you could just have a look first—just in case there's anything useful."

There was a long pause. "Lily, you do realize you sound absolutely insane, don't you?"

Your gift will frighten the wary. I fought hard to try and still my mind. I could not afford to alienate Stephen. "Yes. I understand that to you, this is all insane, but psychic phenomena are real, whether you want to admit it or not. You can't deny what happened this summer, how I knew Professor Briggs was a thief, how I learned Amisihathor's story, how you had the dream that saved my life. I know you *want* to deny it and you want me to as well, but it can't be dismissed."

Stephen shook his head, but I went on.

"I *am* a psychic, and I can't make it go away. You've got to accept me for what I am or wash your hands of me. Just please don't do it right now. I need help. Lock me up with Mom later, but don't let Jacob and Rose hurt anyone I love. I know I can trust you. Please."

There was still hesitation in his eyes, but I knew Stephen, and he didn't let me down. "All right. If it will make you rest easier, I'll look at the book. Then I'm handing it over to Jason."

"Thank you. Thank you for being so wonderful. Be careful. I've deactivated the box by touching it, but the book may have some energy too. Just flip through it to see if there are any medicinal plants or recipes. Don't stop to read anything that seems…disturbing, okay?"

He got it out and turned to the first page. "'My name is Rose Adams—'"

A cold breeze blew through the room even though no doors or windows were open and there was no natural source for it. I started, and Stephen looked up in surprise.

"Never mind!" I exclaimed. "Close it! She's near again. Put it back in the box. We can't give her any fuel."

He did as I said, and the chill subsided.

"I was hoping for more time, but she's waiting." I wrapped the blanket tightly around me. "She's out there, Stephen. Has the moon risen yet?"

"I don't know. There are trees in the way."

"Well check the newspaper please!"

He looked around for it. "I cleaned before Jenny came. I'm not sure where I put it."

"Under the chair cushion."

"How did you know?" he asked when he discovered it there.

"Because that's always been your idea of cleaning. Heaven only knows what's under this sofa."

"I am *not* a slob, if that's what you're implying."

"Moonrise!" I demanded.

"Humph." Stephen rustled the pages, still appearing disgruntled; I actually preferred that to his solicitous doubt. "Ten thirty."

"That means it won't be very high in the sky until after eleven. I think that's when they're planning the ceremony."

I saw him open his mouth to ask what ceremony, but just then the doorbell rang. Katy came rushing in like a leaf blown by the wind.

"What is going on here? Lily, what happened to you? Stephen, what's wrong with Lily? Where is Cal? What's he done? Why do I need protection? Lily, are you all right?"

"No, she's not all right," Stephen said, stating the obvious. "Just hold your horses. I'm trying to calm her down. Come out here with me a minute."

They went into the bedroom and closed the door. I could still hear occasional outbursts of "What?!" and "Caliman?!" from Katy over Stephen's low murmur. Then it was Stephen uttering the exact same words. "What?! Caliman?!"

Katy's voice grew softer. Then Stephen spoke again. "That's crazy! How could you let her? After everything that's happened! Merciful God, I can't believe it."

Katy, sounding a little defiant, said, "You can't ignore the truth!"

And Stephen, more loudly, spoke, "She's mixed up with a bunch of psychotics!"

The bedroom door flew open. "We're leaving right now," Stephen announced. "The sooner we get to the police, the better."

Katy had tears in her eyes. "Oh, Lily, I can't bear it that Cal tried to hurt you. I'm so sorry. I never suspected. He seemed so… Are you really sure?"

"Of course I'm sure," I retorted, unable in my fear to worry about her romantic feelings. "I wasn't in the park with an evil twin. Well, I was in a way, but…oh, never mind. We've got to stop Rose and Jacob if we're going to help Cal."

Stephen put his arm around my shoulders so I could lean on him and stand. Katy brought up the rear of our little procession, carrying the iron box. Stephen grimaced when we went outside and he saw Cal's car, but to his credit, he said nothing. He bundled me into the back seat of his own red corvette and got in front with Katy beside him.

"So this is the book that's caused all the trouble?" she said. "It's heavy!"

"You can't imagine *how* heavy," I replied.

"How much of it did you get to read?"

"Not enough…but too much." I lapsed into a brooding silence, and Katy left me alone.

When we reached my house, I was afraid to see what might be happening, but to my relief everything looked normal.

"I'll go in and check, then come and get you," Stephen said. A few minutes that seemed like hours passed before Stephen reappeared. "It's okay. No one has been in, and Cleo is fine—agitated but fine. I don't understand why Jason's not here yet though."

He helped me in and deposited me in my bed. My precious pet came running into the room and leapt up beside me.

"Oh, my sweetheart," I cried, snuggling her close. I began to cry again. Once I got started, it seemed I would never stop.

Stephen made me swallow two pills, supplied me with tissue and sat rubbing my shoulders. "It's all right. You're safe now," he kept saying.

Safe. A horrible thought suddenly occurred to me. "Stephen! My mom. Call the hospital and tell them not to let anyone they don't know into her room. I wouldn't put it past Cal to try and get to me through her. He won't leave me alone as long as he thinks I can help him find that book. Please call now."

Stephen had given up arguing with me. When he got off the phone, I gave him the box. "Take it and put it down in the basement," I pleaded. "Cover it up with anything you can find."

"I'm going to make some hot chocolate," Katy said.

"Lock the doors first…and the windows too!"

I huddled in the bed with Cleo and pulled the covers over my head. Suddenly I felt her stiffen beside me. She let out a low growl, and a thrill of horror went through me. I could hear a low moaning outside the window. Terrified to look but unable not to, I turned over slowly and gazed through the glass.

The red eyes of a great gray wolf stared back at me.

Chapter Sixteen

Cleocatra jumped down from the bed and ran to face him, her back arched, her fur bristling and her teeth bared. The wolf actually stepped back a pace, growling.

"Stephen! Katy!" I yelled. "Get in here!"

They both came running. "What? What's wrong?" Stephen asked.

"The wolf. It's here! It's looking for me. Did you lock everything up?"

"A wolf? Where?" Stephen spun around as if expecting to see it sitting in the chair.

"Right—" I pointed at the window, but the animal was gone. "Well, it was there a second ago!" I insisted. "Just look at Cleo!"

She was swiping at the glass with her paws, still hissing.

"I'm sure there was *something* there," Stephen said cautiously, but I stopped him. "No, it wasn't a husky or a pig or a unicorn either! Now will you please go and make sure this house is secure?"

More with a look of mollifying me than with any conviction, he left to do so. Katy sat down on the bed beside me. Before she could even open her mouth I said, "I'm sorry, Katy. I know how you feel about Cal, but he's not Cal anymore. I think Jacob has taken him over. He wants the book so he can bring Rose back to life."

"There is nothing more important than that book, Lily."

The tone of Katy's voice was chilling. For a moment I didn't even recognize her.

"How could you think of betraying your family this way? How could you forfeit lifetimes of learning and lore? Do you care nothing for the injustices done or your own happiness? Only a fool puts her fate into the hands of others."

"I don't want happiness that causes suffering. It's not right."

"Right and wrong. What petty concepts. It is *right* to be happy and *wrong* to suffer."

"There's more to life than happiness, Rose."

"You dare tell me that? Me, who has endured such pain? Have a care, child. Help Jacob with the Summoning, and our family shall be strong again! You owe it to us. You owe it to yourself and your daughters."

"I can't. I won't!"

The voice took on a wheedling note. "Yet you were tempted. I saw it in your mind. I see it there even now. Everything I promised may yet be yours. Think on it, Lily. Imagine—"

Cleocatra had turned from the window and was coming towards Katy. All at once my cat lunged at my friend and bit her on the ankle.

Katy gave a little scream and kicked out, but Cleo was too quick, and the foot aimed at her head missed.

Stephen came back into the room, and Cleo jumped up into his arms. "What's the matter now?" he asked in confusion.

"She bit me." Katy pointed to her bleeding foot. "Cleo bit me for no reason at all."

No reason except that you were possessed.

"I'm so sorry," I said carefully. "She just doesn't understand what's going on, and it scares her to see me like this. There's some antiseptic in the bathroom. Go check and see how bad the bite is."

Katy left.

Stephen put Cleo down on the bed next to me.

"It wasn't her fault," I said. She was only trying to protect me."

"From *Katy*?"

"No, from Rose. That was her just now, wanting me to give up the book. She can get inside people's minds and speak through them. Poor Katy is close to Cal, so she's probably the easiest to take over." A frown crossed my face. "But how are we going to keep Katy safe and make sure she's really herself?"

"I'll keep an eye on her. If she starts acting strangely, I can give her a sedative. It's a good thing I brought my bag. You ought to be feeling pretty sleepy yourself by now."

"I guess there's too much adrenaline, but I am calmer. I would so love to sleep! But I can't—not until I'm sure everything's all right."

"Okay. I'll take care of Katy first. Then I'll call Jason again. I locked up, I checked with the hospital, and there's no sign of a wolf. So try to relax. I'll be right back."

I hugged Cleocatra close. "Thank you," I whispered. She purred and rubbed her face against mine. "We're going to be safe, Cleo. No one's going to get us. Don't worry."

Katy soon returned. "Stephen bandaged me up. The way he kept looking at me, you'd think he was afraid I was going into shock." She sat on the bed as far from my cat as she could get. "I'm glad Cleo's had all her shots, because she really got me. What on Earth made her act that way?"

"Nothing on *Earth*," I replied. "She wasn't biting you at all. She was biting Rose."

"What do you mean? *I'm* the one with tooth marks and blood on me!"

"What were we talking about when it happened?"

Katy frowned. "I don't know exactly. Stephen and I were checking the doors and windows, and then you yelled. We came in to see what was wrong, and then she bit me."

"You don't remember trying to get the book?"

"Of course not, because I didn't."

"Katy, you…changed. Your voice, even your face, were different. You demanded that I give you the book. That's when Cleo came after you. She knew it *wasn't* you. After she bit you, you tried to kick her. Then you snapped out of it. I guess it was the pain."

"Good Lord, Lily! I don't remember anything except realizing that my ankle hurt and I was bleeding. Are you saying Rose took over?"

"Only for a few minutes. After all, your mind must be in a lot of turmoil right now. But you have to be on guard. She could try it again. You have the power to keep her out. Concentrate on things that are important to you. Think of your family. Remember happy times. Or maybe Stephen can just give you a sedative."

"That sounds like the best idea. Right now I'm afraid all that concentrating might make my head explode."

"Do I ever know the feeling." I gave a huge yawn. "I need to sleep. Come on, Katy. Make up with Cleo. She didn't want to hurt you. Did you, sweetness?"

Katy reached out a hand tentatively, and Cleo licked it. Then she rubbed along Katy's arm, purring.

"See? She's apologizing," I said. "She only wanted to bring you back."

"Well, I guess I forgive you then." Katy ran her hands over Cleo's fur. "It *did* hurt though!"

"I wonder," I said, trying hard to keep my eyes open, "if I should call the others in the group. I can't believe they all know Cal's crazy. They should be warned. And they could help us too. The more minds we have standing against Rose, the better."

"How can we be sure though? Maybe you can warn them, but I don't know if I'd trust any of them to come over here and fight for you."

I thought a moment. "Maybe *you* could call them. You've met them all. Have Stephen give you the sedative and stay with you. We'll be safe once we're asleep."

"Okay. I'll tell Jo and get her to pass it along. Happy dreams."

"And to you." I couldn't hold out any longer. With Cleo cradled in the crook of my arm, I surrendered to sweet oblivion.

A sharp pain awakened me some time later. Struggling through layers of unconsciousness, I heard Cleo making a noise that would have woken the dead. Dimly, I became aware that there was blood on my arm and that Cleo must have scratched me. She began butting me with her head. Seeing that my eyes were open, she jumped onto the floor and ran to the door, where she stood staring at me, howling insistently.

Something was wrong. "Stephen?" I called out weakly. "Katy?"

Cleocatra howled louder. Clearly she expected me to get up.

I swung my legs over the side of the bed and fought back the waves of dizziness washing over me. Staggering to the door, I called again. "Stephen?"

The silence brought fear flooding through me, which served to make me more alert. I crept into the living room. Katy was sound asleep on the sofa, Stephen was nowhere to be seen, and someone was ringing the doorbell.

I froze, leaning against the wall. I had the absurd notion to send Cleo to see who it was—or maybe not so absurd. My pet was already making her way over there. She sat down and looked at me, no longer hissing but as calm as an ancient statue.

I inched my way along to the curtains, where I carefully peered outside. Jo and Derek were standing there, looking extremely worried. I glanced at Cleo. She meowed mildly, as if to indicate they were safe visitors.

Derek called out, "Lily! Lily, are you all right?"

Cleo inclined her head towards the door. *Let them in!*

I spoke to the couple outside. "I'm really not feeling well."

"We know," Derek answered. "Katy called and told us about Cal. We just want to help, and I think you're going to need us."

"Stephen is here," I said, although by now my stomach was in knots with worry over him. "Katy too."

"Good," Jo replied. "The more there are to fight him, the better."

I made up my mind. I needed help, and I felt I could trust them. I opened up the door.

"Lily, you don't look well at all!" were Jo's first words. "You should be in bed." She caught sight of the figure on the sofa. "Is she all right?"

"She's just sleeping. I was too, until Cleo woke me up." I looked down at my arm. "She wanted to make sure I knew you were here."

"Good girl," Derek said, stooping to pet her.

Cleo brushed against his leg.

I swayed a little on my feet, and Jo reached to steady me. "You'd better lie back down. Derek, lock the door again. Where is Stephen anyway?"

"I don't know. I haven't seen him since before I went to sleep. He should have heard all this commotion. Will you look for him please?"

"Sure. Let's get you into bed first." Derek picked me up and carried me back to my room.

I could hear Jo going through the house calling Stephen's name.

"Do you need something for your arm?" Derek asked.

"I usually just put antiseptic on. There's some in the bathroom. Stephen used it on Katy."

"What have you got, a cat or a tiger?" It was good to see someone smile.

"I've got the latest incarnation of a long line going back to ancient Bubastis," I said proudly. "Cleo is no ordinary cat."

"I believe you." Derek went and found the antiseptic and sprayed some on the scratch. Jo came into the room with Cleo trailing behind her. Her face was worried. "Stephen's not here. I couldn't find a note either."

"But that's impossible. He wouldn't have left us. Something's happened to him!"

"You don't know that for sure," Jo said, trying to soothe me. "He could have just stepped out for a minute—"

"Not with Cal running around." I reached for the telephone and with shaking fingers dialed Stephen's cell. There was no answer, and panic gripped me.

"He's not picking up!"

"He's a doctor, isn't he?" Jo asked sensibly. "Try his pager."

How could I have forgotten his pager? I dialed the phone again, left a message and waited. I nearly cried with relief when at last I heard Stephen's voice. "Thank God you're all right! Why did you go? I was worried sick!"

"I got called in, Lily. They said there was an emergency with Sandy. Where's Jason? Why are you even awake?"

"Jason?" I echoed in confusion.

Stephen's voice suddenly became tense. "Jason's not there?"

"Derek and Jo are here. They came after Katy called them. There's no Jason."

"Lily, Jason was two minutes away from your house when I left. What could have happened to him?"

I heard the anxiety in Stephen's voice, and it heightened my own. "I don't know. You'd better check on him. Katy and I are all right here with Derek and Jo."

"And how do you know you can trust them? That whole coven could be in on this!"

"They're not a coven," I said, "and they've been here for a while, helping. Cleo likes them. It's okay."

"Well, I'll be back as soon as I can. I'll page Jason now, and I'm calling more police to come over. Put Derek or Jo on the phone."

I handed the receiver to Jo, who listened for a minute and then hung up. "The doctor says stay in bed, keep warm and drink plenty of fluids. Katy should sleep for a while. Also, if we harm one hair on your head, he will personally kill us."

"Sorry," I said. "He's just worried. He sent over a policeman friend who never got here."

"Maybe there was some kind of emergency, like the kind that called Stephen to the hospital." Derek's face was grim.

My eyes widened. "Could Cal do that?"

"With Rose's energy, I'd say yes. There's more going on than we ever dreamt of."

He exchanged a glance with Jo but tried to downplay the situation for my sake.

"Look, the police know what's happened. More of them will be coming 'round soon, and so will Stephen. We're here with you. Cal would be mad to think he could just burst in and take you away."

"But Rose can get inside people's minds. You don't know what she could make you do."

Jo put her hand on my shoulder. "We can protect ourselves, Lily, and you can keep them out. You've beaten them once already, right on Rose's home ground. This time we're here to help you."

"I'm so tired," I replied softly.

"And so strong. Look, I know it sounds ridiculous, but try to relax. We'll watch out for Cal. I'm sure the cavalry will be here before he will."

"And they need that book to gain full power," Derek put in. "Without it, I don't think Rose can manifest, so don't worry."

At that exact moment, an eerie noise filled the air.

Chapter Seventeen

We all jumped. Cleocatra's hackles rose. I looked wildly towards the window. "The wolf!"

Sure enough, its face was pressed against the glass for all the world, as if it were going to spring right through. Derek and Jo sat down on each side of me and grabbed a hand.

"Don't look at it," Jo warned. "You know what to do, Lily. Call down the light. Imagine it protecting you. Imagine everyone you've ever loved protecting you. Put up your shield."

I concentrated with all my might. My body started to feel warm, and my mind began to detach itself. It was working! I could sense the energies of Jo and Derek and what felt like a flow of electricity between me and Cleocatra. "We ask for protection," Derek was saying. "Keep us in the light and keep any evil from entering this house. Give us strength. Give us power. Please keep us safe."

I imagined a wall around us, holding all the warmth and blessings in. When I opened my eyes, the wolf was gone, but the danger was not. It was lurking outside like an amorphous black cloud. Cold began to seep into the room. The very atmosphere began to weigh down on us. I started to shake.

Derek took my arm. "Keep concentrating, Lily. Remember the light."

"Katy," I gasped. "We have to make sure she's all right."

With Jo on one side and Derek on the other, we rose and went into the living room. Katy was still on the sofa, seemingly asleep, but when I looked more closely at her face, it was a strange, unhealthy color. Her breath was shallow and irregular. Icy terror washed over me.

"What have you done?"

Give him the book. Only give him the book, and no one will be hurt.

"No, no! Leave her alone. Get away!" I shouted to the voice in my head.

Banging started on the front door. "Let me in, Lily!" Cal called. "Let me in! Only I can help Katy."

"Don't open that door, whatever you do!" Jo knelt down beside Katy and held both her hands. "Take this spirit off her! You have no right to touch this person. Leave her!"

I flung myself down and put my head on Katy's chest. "Please protect her," I prayed. I pictured her in a circle of magic flames that no one could cross. A terrible pain jolted through me. In that moment I felt Rose's horror, and I knew I had my weapon. "Fire! Think of fire. We're in the center of a circle, and the flames are burning all around. For us, they're a shelter and a shield. But to Rose, they mean death. She can't cross into the fire!"

Derek and Jo obeyed me, and I could feel the renewed energy. Katy's breathing evened out again. Cal went silent. With trembling hope, I lifted my head. Then we all heard the sound of the door opening.

"It's not enough," I said frantically. "He's getting in!"

Jo and Derek rushed off. I could hear shouting and scuffling, but I didn't dare leave Katy. I had to keep envisioning the circle of fire around her. Before long, it grew quiet. I looked up, expecting to see Jo and Derek.

But it was Cal who stood at the door to the living room. "So, Lily," he asked, almost conversationally, "where is the book?"

I gaped at him for a moment, then stammered, "Wh-what did you do to Jo and Derek?"

"Your guardians? They are unconscious on the floor. I did not even need sorcery. The people of this day are weak."

Defiance rose up in me. "You can't have the book!"

His jaw twitched angrily. "I did not credit *your* strength, although I should have. I will not make that mistake again. Tell me what you have done with the book, or your friends here will pay the price."

I was incredulous. "You'd really kill three people just to get your hands on a book?"

"Not *a* book—*the* book. Once I read it and can bring Rose back, we can be together again. Nothing will be beyond our reach. We can overcome death itself. We will be able to understand and direct the course of the cosmos!"

Lily, give him the book. I do not want to hurt you. The Summoning requires your blood, only a little. Do not force Jacob to take it without your consent.

They literally need my blood? And I'd thought all the references to it were family related. My mind raced. *What can I do? If I leave with him, will my friends be safe? Or will Rose sweep in and destroy them?*

I had to play for time. I couldn't let him take me, or else he would have the book and my blood, and I'd probably be dead. *Dear God, what should I do?*

Cal gave my arm a vicious wrench. "Hurry up, or I will choke Katy myself."

I tried to control my fear. "Where is my cat?"

"That hell-beast? I threw her in the closet, and I hope she suffocates. If I did not have the protection of these clothes, my skin would be scraped raw. Now give me the book, or these people shall die."

I didn't know if he and Rose were powerful enough to actually carry out the threat, but I couldn't take a chance. "It's in the basement," I said with resignation.

"Then fetch it!"

He practically dragged me down the stairs. I looked around at the boxes in storage and all my holiday decorations. They seemed to belong in one of Cal's parallel universes. "Where is it?" he demanded as I hesitated.

"I don't know! Stephen brought it down." I began searching and found it under a Christmas tree skirt.

Cal took it and caressed it with a smile. "It is ours, Rose! It is ours at last!" he said in a voice ringing with triumph.

He forced me up the basement steps and out into the night.

I almost collided with a figure on the front porch before I recognized her. "Yvette!"

She gave me a cold look and turned to Cal. "We've got to hurry!"

He opened the back door of Yvette's car and shoved me in. He and Yvette got in the front. My heart sank even further. If the police had put up roadblocks, they would have been meant for my vehicle or Cal's. They wouldn't have been looking for Yvette's license plate. *What chance do I have now, against the two of them?*

I tried reasoning with Yvette. "You can't want to be a part of this. Jo and Derek and Katy are unconscious inside that house. Cal has already threatened to kill them, and now he's kidnapping me. You'll go to prison!"

"Oh, I don't think so," Cal replied. "Now that we've got the book, no one can touch us. Rose was one of the most powerful witches who ever lived. Her journal is full of her knowledge, including how to bring her back. With what she can teach us, we'll be able to go anywhere, to do anything we want."

"And the first thing on the list is getting married." Yvette was as proud as a lioness bringing down her prey.

"Naturally. I told you I was just using Katy."

"I knew all along. How could you possibly prefer her to me? I was glad when you called and asked me to come with you. Putting up with her was very tiresome."

"Yvette, don't you realize he is not really Cal anymore? It's Jacob! He doesn't care about you. He only wants to bring Rose back so he can be with *her*."

"Of course that's what you'd say," Yvette jeered, "but I think I know Cal a lot better than you do."

By now we were speeding down the road. The miles disappeared under our wheels while my mind turned almost as quickly, trying to come up with something, anything that would keep me from giving in to despair. All I could do for the time being was huddle in the seat and wait. *Once we get to wherever we were going and out on open ground, maybe I'll have a chance to—*

The car suddenly slowed down. "There's something in the road!" Yvette cried. "Hold on!"

The brakes squealed, the car swerved, and Yvette wrenched at the wheel, swearing loudly. To my horror, we were sliding onto the shoulder, right towards a tree. I wrapped my arms around the headrest in front of me and held on for dear life.

Yvette managed to slow the car and turn it enough so we didn't plow head on into the tree, but we slid sideways so that the right side took most of the impact. After we screeched to a halt, we sat for a minute, stunned. "Cal, are you all right?" Yvette asked, struggling with her airbag.

There was no answer. Cal's bag had not deployed, and he'd banged his head against the dashboard.

"He's unconscious. Lily, are you okay?"

I couldn't reply at first. Then I mumbled, "I guess so." *As if you care.*

"Then quick! Help me get him into the trunk."

I was sure I could not be hearing her right. *Did I hit my head too?* But Yvette was already getting out of the car and yanking my door open. "Hurry! You take his arms, and I'll take his legs."

"In the trunk?" I repeated stupidly.

"Where else? We've got to make sure he's out of commission when he wakes up, and we need to get back to your house as quickly as we can."

I was amazed at her coolness. She acted as if things like that happened every day. I climbed out of the car in a fog. "Why are you helping me?"

I saw her poise crack for the first time. "We're all in big trouble, thanks to you. You had to investigate that damned portrait and start communing with a black witch. Cal felt obligated to rally round and drag everyone else in too—only the others were luckier. They're not as brilliant, not as psychic, not as..." Her voice faltered. "...vulnerable." She was speaking as she opened the front side door. "Come on. Help me! And be careful."

Together we pulled Cal out of the car and lifted him into Yvette's trunk. It still seemed unreal to me, but the ache in my arm and shoulder testified that it wasn't. "He-he'll be all right, won't he?"

"I sure as hell hope so." Yvette took off her jacket and put it under Cal's head. Then she pressed her palm against his cheek, just as I had with Kent when I was overwhelmed by tenderness. "I'm sorry," she whispered and shut the lid.

We got back into the car, which started immediately in spite of its collision with the tree. "Can't beat a Lexus," Yvette remarked as we took off.

I was still trying to make sense of all of it. "Why didn't his airbag work?"

"Because I disabled it. I aimed for his side of the car and slowed down enough to make sure we'd all be in one piece."

"So there was nothing in the road?"

"Nothing."

"You could have killed us!"

"It was a calculated risk. I suppose you'd have come up with a better plan? Like hitting Cal with a shovel?"

I ignored that. "You knew he'd been taken over?"

"Didn't I try to tell you when we met in the park that something was wrong? He didn't close his mind to me because of you or Katy. He was trying to hide the presence of Rose and Jacob, and he did a damn good job. With everyone concentrating on the two of them, no one had the energy to question Cal's actions."

Least of all me, I thought dismally.

"When he called tonight and asked me to run away with him, of course I realized it wasn't Cal speaking. As much as I would have liked to believe he suddenly wanted to marry me, I knew it was really about the book. He's been obsessed with finding it. I had to discover what was happening for myself. The trip to your house pretty much explained that."

"I was afraid he would kill us," I said with a tremor.

"Not *Cal*. He's a good man, and it's not his fault that this has happened." She didn't have to say, *"It's yours."* The words hung in the air between us.

"They aren't completely integrated yet." I tried to sound hopeful. "That's why Cal can still talk in his own voice sometimes, the way he did with you. Rose and Jacob need his mind. They can't fully manifest without his help. We'll stop them from using the book and banish them. Then Cal will be back to normal."

"Oh really? It's that easy? What makes you think we'll be *able* to banish them?"

"We have the book. Rose isn't strong enough to hold Jo, Derek and Katy once we get there, especially with Cal unconscious. She doesn't have enough energy to fight all the people coming into the house."

"I wouldn't be too sure of that. She's fed off Cal's energy for a while now. And we supplied it too, communicating with her and going to where she lived. All the negative emotions of tonight will only have added to it. Also, she has the full moon, her birth moon, and a living relative to draw from."

"I'll never help her again!"

"No? I hope not." Yvette shot me a speculative glance. "What's in that book anyway?"

My foot was resting right beside it, and I hurriedly pulled back. "Horrible things. Rose was bent on power and revenge. She killed Thomas after she fell in love with Jacob, and I don't know how many others her poisons affected. She said she 'assisted' the villagers."

"So no boon to mankind?" Yvette's tone was acidic.

I hesitated. "No one has read the whole thing. There probably are treatments for illness and injury. She had to be able to help her family and anyone willing to pay her."

"Ah yes, family."

I wished Yvette would stop looking at me with that appraising aspect.

"Didn't she promise to spare you? Make all of your dreams come true or something?"

"She did." I felt I owed Yvette honesty. "I'm not going to pretend she didn't tempt me. What if *your* life was turned upside down and a persuasive voice started whispering in your ear? Wouldn't you want everything made right? Wouldn't you want your mother healed and the man you love by your side again? Wouldn't you want your artistic ability reclaimed and a great job? Rose vowed to stop the dark magic. She said

Cal would be realizing his greatest dream by sharing her knowledge. She was...hypnotic."

"Then how did you resist her?"

"Fairy stones."

"What? Like the ones from Cal's childhood?"

"Yes. There were some lying in the grass, and I caught sight of them. I remembered his story, and I knew I couldn't let him be hurt, no matter what. I like to believe I would have stopped Rose anyway, but...well, that clinched it."

A new respect had dawned in Yvette's eyes. "That was no small feat, turning away from someone so powerful. I'm glad you did it."

"I'm glad you showed up tonight."

And that was the closest we were going to get to complimenting each other.

I was silent as we drove the rest of the way. I didn't know what we'd find when we returned. I hoped Yvette was wrong and that Rose would be weaker.

We could see the lights and cars before we even reached the house. Stephen and Amy, along with four policemen, were our welcoming committee.

Stephen grabbed me when I got out of the car and hugged me so hard that my arm and shoulder pain doubled. "Thank God, Lily! Where have you been? We could see Derek and Jo through the bedroom window but no sign of you. How did you get out? What are you doing with her?" He nodded towards Yvette. "And where is Jones? Is he the one who did this?"

"Cal," I answered, just in time for the approaching policeman to hear, "is in the trunk of Yvette's car."

"That damaged vehicle right there, ma'am?" the lawman asked. "Are you saying there's a body in there?"

"Oh, he's still alive. We just put him in there after we crashed to make sure he was out of the way."

"After you crashed?" Stephen held me out at arm's length and looked at me with a critical eye. "Are you hurt?"

"No, but I'm afraid Cal might be. Why are we all standing out here? Who's helping Katy and Jo and Derek?"

"I'll need a full account of what's happened," the officer said, beckoning two more policemen over. "Are you able to give one now, ma'am?" he asked as the others went to open Yvette's trunk.

"Let me make sure she's all right first," Stephen said indignantly. "She might have some trauma."

Ambulance workers joined the policemen at Yvette's car. They lifted Cal onto a stretcher, and Yvette walked along beside him.

Stephen led me over to his own vehicle. "Sit down in here and let me have a look at you," he said.

"Stephen, I'm okay. I want to go inside. You let Cleo out of the closet, didn't you? I'm sure she hated being stuck in there. How are the others? Why haven't they taken them to the hospital yet?"

Stephen looked uneasy. He lowered his voice. "Lily, we can't get inside the house."

Chapter Eighteen

I stared at him. "What do you mean? Why not?"

"None of the keys will work—not mine, not the ones the police have, and not even the extra one you keep hidden in the hydrangeas. They fit, but they won't turn. We tried breaking the glass, and it won't shatter. It's like it's made of rock. They finally took the hinges off the front door, but it still won't budge. And the closer we get to the house, the colder it gets. It's absolutely freezing at the threshold."

"Rose," I breathed. "Rose has taken over the house, and everyone is still in there!"

"Wait a minute." Stephen tried to stop me as I began climbing out of the car. "Where do you think you're going?"

"To get the others. We have to fight ice with fire."

"Lily, wait!"

But I was already out and approaching the group around Yvette, who was bringing them all up to speed. "Rose has put up a barrier," I explained when she had finished. "No one can get inside the house to help. We have to do something."

"We'll link our energies." Yvette looked to Stephen. "Is Cal still unconscious?"

"Yes," Stephen replied. He had followed along behind me after consulting with the EMTs. "They're taking him to the hospital now. What do you mean, link your energies?"

"Don't tell him," I said. "It will only upset him. Is your friend Jason here?"

"We found him a block away, out cold in his patrol car. I brought him around, but he doesn't remember what happened. Sandy didn't really need me either. I never should have left you, Lily. I'm so sorry."

"Don't be silly. You didn't know. And anyway, if you'd stayed, you'd be stuck inside the house now too. Can Jason hold off the other policemen until we try to break through?"

"You can't get through," Stephen insisted. "We've all tried."

"You just didn't know *what* to try. We need some fire. Anything will do. Does anyone have matches or a cigarette lighter?"

Yvette produced a gold lighter. "A bonfire," she said. "That will give us an image to focus on and be a horrific symbol for Rose."

Lily, NO! You cannot! It is murder!

I tried to ignore her. "Stephen, can you please ask Jason if that's all right? Tell him we need to do it to fight the cold. It's the only way we'll get in. After that we'll answer all their questions, but we have to help the others first."

Stephen shook his head. "I'll try." He walked away like a man on a doomed mission.

The rest of us started to make a pile for the bonfire, with everyone giving advice.

"Remember to call down the light."

"Center yourself."

"Try to block out the emotions and concentrate."

"Think of the fire. Picture it warming the whole house and the people inside."

"Picture them waking up and being fine."

"Picture the flames around Rose, taking her power."

We built it in front of the bedroom window, through which Derek and Jo could still be seen, lying on the floor. As we did, Stephen came back with Jason.

"Since it's this or a SWAT team, we're going to let you give it a try," Jason said, "but we've called a fire truck for backup. We have to keep the blaze contained."

Another policeman approached us. "Do I understand that you're having some kind of exorcism here?"

"Well…sort of," I answered hesitantly, waiting for the ridicule.

To my surprise, none came. Instead the man said, "Do you need more help? I'm involved in a ghost-hunting group, and I've had experience with this kind of thing."

I certainly hadn't expected it, and neither had Stephen or Jason. Their mouths practically fell open.

Yvette said, "Surprise, surprise. We're in all walks of life. Thank you, Officer…?"

"Mitch," he supplied. And to Jason, "No need to go telling everybody, is there? I wouldn't want my credibility questioned."

"Hey, your private life is your own," Jason replied. He and Stephen left while we briefed Mitch on the situation.

"It's too bad we don't have a priest," our new recruit said. "Although they're very shy about this nowadays."

"We'll just have to make do. We've got to work while Cal is still unconscious. Otherwise, he'll give her strength," I pointed out.

"Okay, Lily, get the book," Yvette directed.

I returned to the car, took out the iron box, and brought it back.

Yvette opened it up and took out the leather-bound tome. She and the others silently turned the pages. After what seemed a very long time, Yvette spoke. "There are some spells for healing in here, including natural remedies, but it's far too risky to copy them. We can't carry on Rose's work in any way."

"Are you sure?" In spite of everything, I still found myself reluctant to destroy the volume.

"Yes, Lily, I'm sure." She pinned me with her gaze. "The death and destruction are much stronger. Even the good is tainted by her hand. We have to put it on the fire and break Rose's power forever. Are you going to be able to help? Because if you fight against us, even subconsciously, we probably won't succeed."

My daughter! My own flesh! Surely you cannot do this!

"I have to," I said out loud. "I have no choice. This evil cannot be brought into the world."

Amy put her arm around me. "I know you can do this, Lily.

Yvette nodded. "I trust you."

I drew a deep breath. "I won't let you down."

"Then we need some bigger branches." Yvette was all business. "There's no telling how long we may have to sustain this."

We wandered around my yard searching. It was easy enough to see, with the police lights and the moon.

The moon.

I tilted back my head. There it was, shining in full splendor—Rose's birth moon…and mine.

More fuel was brought. "That should do it," Yvette said. "Now let's go over this. We must coordinate our thoughts."

We practiced until the fire truck arrived. Then we gathered around the pyre and laid the book atop it. The sound of axes rang in our ears, but a glance showed that the firemen were making no progress getting into the house.

"I'm going to start slowly," Yvette said. Despite her profession of trust, she was eyeing me warily. She flicked her lighter and touched it to the edge of a page. The tiny flame immediately went out.

There was a moment of anxious silence.

"Get the wood burning first, then put the book in," Mitch suggested.

Yvette hesitated. "That might not be a good idea."

"Why not?"

"If you must know, I'm worried about Lily."

"I told you, I'm on your side!"

"I know, but it doesn't hurt to be careful. We're not sure what's going to happen."

"You mean you're not sure if you can depend on me," I retorted. "Well I started all this, and I'm strong enough to finish!"

Yvette didn't look happy, but she opened the lighter again. This time, she held it under the twigs directly beneath the heavy volume. They flared up with a crackle. Smoke curled around the cover.

"NO!" I screamed.

Everyone's attention was riveted on me. Yvette grabbed the book off the fire. I stood cringing, with my hands over my face. I was finding it hard to breathe.

"*That's* why I was worried." Yvette took me by the elbow and steered me away. "Lily," she said gently but firmly, "you are in no physical danger. No matter how it feels, there's nothing wrong with you. Your skin is cool. Your lungs are clear. I can see you, and you are *not* burning. Open your eyes. Open them!" She pried my fingers apart.

I blinked at her, still gasping.

"The Earth is under your feet. The night air is all around you. Concentrate. Recite the alphabet backwards. Come on. Z-Y-X…"

I tried as hard as I could, but I still felt stunned. "W-W-W…" My voice trailed off ineffectually.

"Okay, tell me the rulers of Egypt. King Tut. Cleopatra. Who came after them?"

My mind reached out and latched on to a mental image of Kent. "The Romans. Conquered the Etruscans. Conquered Egypt too." My racing heart slowed. "Cleopatra was the last pharaoh. After she died, Egypt became a Roman province."

"Good! You're doing very well. Understand, Lily, that what you felt was not *your* memory. You are here, with us, in the physical world. You're safe. What you experienced was sympathetic magic. Like it or not, Rose is your relative. There's a connection between you. When the book is destroyed and she is cast out, it's going to affect you. I'm sorry. I wish you didn't have to do this, but you do."

"What?" I asked, horrified. "Suffer with her?"

Yvette could never be accused of sugarcoating the truth. "It won't be easy or pleasant, but you have power of your own. You have to try to take control. Summon every ounce of courage and conviction you possess, because that woman is your enemy." She gripped me by the shoulders to emphasize her words.

"Rose is slowly killing your friends right now. She's done her best to rob Cal of his sanity, and she doesn't have any respect for yours either. She will say or do anything to protect herself. You cannot listen. You saw the book. You know the crimes she's committed."

I swallowed hard. I was petrified, but I knew that what Yvette said was true. No matter what it took, Rose had to be banished. I went back to the group.

"You have to disown her. She has no right to hurt you. Start with that," Yvette instructed. "Here. Put your hand on the book."

I did so with great reluctance. Lightning bolts of pain shot through me as soon as I touched it.

You foolish child! You are throwing away your inheritance and any chance at happiness! You would destroy the past and the future of your own family?

"You are NOT my family," I answered through gritted teeth. "No relation of mine would kill or injure anyone."

Oh really? Then what of your mother? What of you!

"I claim neither kith nor kin!" The words came unbidden to my lips. "May Heaven ensure you perish utterly and all of your evil with you!"

Yvette took the book. "Well done, Lily. I'm going to put it on the fire now. Prepare yourself. Link hands. Feel the might of each other. Begin the blessing."

My throat was raw and my voice hoarse, but I joined in the chant. "We call down the light to bless and protect us. Keep us safe from harm and give us power to conquer this evil. All good spirits, aid us!"

My eyes were stinging, and I began to cough. It felt as if someone were draining me of my life force. I knew the book was burning. I tried desperately to remember my mantra, but it was lost in swirling images of chaos and destruction.

This is madness! This is death, Lily! Mine and yours!

"We ask that you give strength to our sister Lily." Yvette had stepped into the circle. "Clear her mind and free her energy. She is the one chosen to end this. Help her!"

I could no longer think. It was only a stubborn spark deep inside me that kept me on my feet. I wasn't going to let Rose win. Somehow, I had to endure.

Suddenly, I could see a light. It did not burn but bathed me in a comforting glow.

I am here.

Something crucial shifted, as if a gear in the universe had turned. I saw a familiar face that I instantly trusted, a woman whose heart was speaking to mine.

I shoulder this burden with you, Lily, and we shall throw off its yoke together. You are not our family's destruction but its salvation. The good lives on in you. The wickedness shall die this night forever.

I felt my pain ease. *What have I been searching for? Of course! How could I forget? Daddy, Mom, Kent, Katy, Stephen, Cleo, home, safety...* With renewed vigor, I was able to recite the second part of the prayer. "We call for the peace of the innocent and the punishment of the guilty. We command the spirit of Rose Woodbine to leave this plane and disappear into the void forever. GO!"

I could hear Rose crying out in terror, hurling hideous curses; each one hit me like a blow.

Mitch's shirt began to smolder, and Amy slumped forward like a ragdoll.

Anger welled up within me. *Threatening my friends and my family? She will never do that again.* I stared into the fire and pictured it warming those within the house, releasing them from their sleep. I was amazed by the energy I felt coursing through me. I sent an image of those same flames surrounding Rose and consuming her. "OUT!" I cried. "Your power is broken! You are naught but dust and ashes. GO!"

A low moan came from within the house, rising on the air. I thought I heard a man's agonized shout and the bark of a wolf. Dark clouds passed over the moon as a bitterly cold breeze whooshed by. The moan became a shriek and then a scream, one so horrible that it seemed to be a living force. I felt it batter against me. Then, suddenly, everything was still. There was no sound but the crackling of the leaves.

I lifted my eyes to the window. Derek and Jo were sitting up inside, looking around in a daze. Relief made my knees weaker still. Mitch was already headed off to join his fellow officers. "Thank you," I whispered to my ally. "Thank you for helping me."

An invisible hand brushed back my hair. *It is I who must thank you. You have given me strength. I never had her power, nor the desire for it. Love was my greatest happiness. Thomas has been avenged. Now, at last, the innocent shall know peace, as we have prayed. Do not look back in bitterness but forward in hope. Farewell, true flower of our family. Farewell.*

"Are you all right, Lily?" Yvette was taking my arm. "I've never seen such a close call. You really were incredible."

"I wasn't alone." I discovered that my eyes were full of tears. "She fought with me, for all of us."

"Who?"

The answer came to me in a flash. "Irene. Irene Adams, Rose's older sister."

"I didn't know she had one."

"Her portrait is hanging in the Woodbine house. The first time we went to the park and visited the Woodville cemetery, Cal and I saw her grave. She's buried right next to Thomas. The records mention Amos's daughter, but Irene was his daughter-in-*law*. She wasn't Thomas's sister but his wife. And Susan was *her* child."

"But how can that be?"

I saw the whole story unfold before me. "Irene was the eldest of the three Adams sisters, so she was in line to marry first. She fell in love with Thomas Woodbine. They led a quiet, peaceful life together. She was the opposite of her fiery, beautiful sister, and she wanted nothing to do with the family legacy of magic. Rose was angry with her for turning her back on it and jealous because Irene had made such an advantageous match. Then Irene got pregnant. She and Thomas were so happy." The tears rolled down my cheeks. "But she died right after giving birth, with her baby lying on her breast." I pulled some tissues from my pocket. The residual emotion of that event hit me like a hammer. It was a minute before I could continue. "Susan was the first Woodbine grandchild. Rose knew Amos would never accept her marriage to Jacob or acknowledge any children they had. She also knew Thomas wasn't going to live much longer. So she cast her spell and married him. That gave her custody of Susan."

"Wow." Amy wiped her brow with her sleeve. "And she couldn't even wait for Thomas to die a natural death. I'm glad Susan got away from her."

"So am I," I said fervently. "Elizabeth Adams was more like Irene than Rose. She gave Susan a fresh start in England. At least someone had a happy ending."

It had all clicked into place: the sweet-faced woman at my table in the dream, the warning on the tomb in Hope Cemetery, and Cal falling to the ground when I wasn't even sure my shovel had hit him. It was Irene behind the scenes, trying to help me. I was deeply relieved that it was she, not Rose, who was my direct maternal ancestor.

Stephen appeared and put an arm around my waist. "Come on inside," he said.

Katy was sitting up on the sofa, looking around in a daze.

"Are you okay?" I asked anxiously.

"I'm freezing," my friend replied. "What the hell is going on? I feel like I've been trapped in a nightmare."

"I know, but you're awake now. Let Stephen have a look at you. I'll be right back."

I headed into my bedroom, where Amy and Yvette were fussing over Derek and Jo, and yanked open the louvered closet door. No cat greeted me. "Cleo?" I called in panic. "Cleocatra! Cleo, where are you?"

A noise made me turn my head. It seemed to be coming from under the bed. I fell to the floor and pulled up the dust ruffle. Cleocatra crawled out slowly, and I saw that she was dragging her back leg. "Oh, my baby!" I exclaimed, helping her gingerly. "What happened, my poor little sweetheart?" I nestled her in my lap and kissed her head. "He hurt you, didn't he?" Suddenly my voice rose to a shout. "That bastard!"

"We're all right, Lily," Derek said, looking over at me. "What about you?"

"He hurt my cat!" I wailed.

Stephen came into the room. "What's the matter?"

"That bastard Jacob hurt Cleo!" I sobbed. That was just the final straw.

Stephen stooped down and had a look at her. Cleo let him feel the leg gently. "It's not broken," he said. "Probably just sprained. But we'll take her to the vet tomorrow." He lifted Cleo in one arm and held the other out for me.

I got to my feet shakily. "I've got to get into bed."

"That's a very good idea. I'm afraid you'll have to give a statement first though. Why don't you just lie here for now, and I'll send them in to you."

So I got under the covers, and Stephen put Cleo beside me. It now seemed like some kind of bizarre dream. My bedroom was filled with people. Outside I could see firemen extinguishing the blaze. I petted Cleo and heard her purr, which was reassuring. Derek and Jo came and sat on the end of the bed.

"I'm sorry, Lily," Derek said. "Cal just floored us. He had the strength of a madman."

"You two have no reason to apologize. You tried to protect me. I'm so sorry this happened to you."

"Yvette says he's in the hospital now. She just left to be with him." Derek shrugged helplessly. "Who would have believed it? We all thought we knew him so well."

"You did, until he became someone else."

Jo touched her head gingerly. "We went down like bowling pins. The rest was a dream. I was in a dark cave, and it was freezing cold."

"Me too," Derek said. "We woke up, and everyone was gathered around us. Yvette was saying Rose had been banished. We're still not clear on everything that happened, but I guess we have to talk to the police now."

"And here they come."

To my relief, it was Jason and Mitch. They sent Derek and Jo into the next room while they wrote down my story. Jason raised his eyebrows now and again, but Mitch seemed unfazed.

I was glad when it was over and Katy could come in and join me. I saw that she'd been crying.

"Oh, Lily, I can't believe what's happened!"

I hugged her tightly. "I'm so glad you're all right."

"I guess so. I was just dreaming for what seemed like forever. At first I was floating, but then I felt I could hardly breathe, like something was pressing down on me. I was slowly being crushed. Then it got cold, so cold that I thought I was sleeping in snow. And then I woke up."

"It's all over now. Just like a bad dream, it will fade."

"But what about you? Is it true that Cal kidnapped you? Right here from the house?"

"It's true. If it weren't for Yvette, I don't know what would have happened."

"Yvette." Katy shrugged. "Well, thank God you're safe. I'm sure you don't want to be alone. You can come over to my place."

"Thanks, but I need to be home. You're welcome to stay with me."

"Maybe I will." Katy still seemed to be a little dazed. "But I don't feel like sleeping again for a long time."

Finally, everyone had been interviewed, all questions that could have been asked and answered had been, and the police and fire departments left. "It'll be interesting to see how much of this makes it into the chief's final report," Jason said on the way out. "Something tells me there'll be some editing."

One officer stayed behind to watch the house, since the front door had been unhinged. Stephen decided to stay as well.

The endless day was over at last. And I couldn't wait to fall into a warm, comforting sleep.

Chapter Nineteen

"I can't believe he fooled me!" Katy kept saying in between sobs. "He seemed so perfect!"

"I know, I know," I said soothingly. "He fooled me too. He fooled everyone except for Yvette. Don't feel bad."

"But if it weren't for me, you never would have met him! And then he used me to get to you. Why didn't I see the truth?"

"Katy, a whole group of psychics couldn't see the truth. What chance did you have? Cal is no ordinary person. He's brilliant, and his psychic powers are strong. With Rose lending him her energy, people only saw what he wanted them to see." *Poor Cal. He was as much a victim as anyone else.* "He was all right before he came across her portrait, but she started to feed off him and gradually opened the way for Jacob. Cal had tremendous ambition and the desire to know all the secrets of the universe. Genius can be a heavy burden, especially if you have other issues."

I felt my own burden too, one of guilt. After all, it was through trying to help me that Cal had been exposed to the portrait in the first place.

"He's not a bad person," I insisted. "Rose and Jacob were using him the way he used me. I think they were planning on taking my body for Rose and Cal's for Jacob—permanently." I pushed the horror of that thought to the very back of my mind.

"But he should be all right now. He's got a great lawyer, and he's seeing a psychiatrist. Amy and Derek have taken him to their church for spiritual cleansing. He deserves to get his life back on track. That's why I asked for leniency. Yvette is helping him too."

Katy had no answer for that, but she sniffled. "You're really going to the party? I don't see how you can bear to look at anyone in a witch costume."

"I can bear it because I know it's not real. And I'm going because of the children. Think of how happy it will make them. Did you let me sit alone and pine for Kent? No. And I don't want you to be alone either. Please think about coming. I know how hard it is. I really do. But promise me you'll consider. I don't want to go by myself."

The doorbell rang, and I patted Katy on the shoulder. "I'll be right back," I promised.

Waiting outside was a very woebegone-looking Stephen. "Hi, Lily. I don't want to bother you, but if you've got a few minutes…"

A loud *honk* came from Katy blowing her nose in the bedroom.

"Uh-oh," Stephen said. "Bad timing?"

"I'm trying to calm Katy down. She really liked Cal, you know. But worse, she's blaming herself for letting him into my life, as if it's her fault. I wish I could talk her into coming to the party. I think she'd feel better."

Stephen walked past me and into the bedroom. He sat down beside Katy, who looked at him through watery eyes. "If you don't want to go," he told her, "you can come over and get drunk with me. Then we'll both feel better."

"What's happened?" I asked in surprise. "What about Jenny?"

Stephen sighed. "Jenny is now officially dating Mike Marlowe, one of the top pediatric surgeons. She didn't even have the decency to wait until after the party to tell me."

"Oh, I'm so sorry!" I said, giving him a hug. "I hope it's not my fault. Was it because she got angry when I came running to you?"

"I don't think so. She just had her eye on a higher prize. She dated an intern right before me. She probably won't stop until she gets to the chief of staff."

"Stupid woman. You deserve so much better. And so do you, Katy. Obviously, the two of you have to go together."

"What?" they both said at the same time.

"You've already paid for costumes, right? It's a big social event. Stephen, you have to show Jenny up by bringing a date who's even more beautiful. And Katy, you need to go and have some fun. Must I remind you of the children again? And to be perfectly selfish, I want both of you for company. What do you say?"

They both looked at me and then at each other. "Well..." Katy said slowly. "If you put it that way... What do you think, Stephen?"

"I'm willing if you are," my ever-so-romantic ex replied.

"All right. That's great. You'll be fine as a knight, because Katy is Queen Guinevere. I guess that will make you Lancelot. I'm going solo as Jasmine."

"You can be an exotic dancer we brought from our court!" Katy said, warming to the idea.

"Don't be ridiculous," I said with dignity. "I am a princess."

"I'm a queen. I outrank you, so ha!"

I tossed a pillow at her, glad to see her mood lightening a bit. It had been three days since the horrific events that had befallen us. I'd slept through most of the first two, but now I was no longer tired, Cleo's leg was mending quickly, and I was happy to be safe at home. *If only my two friends felt as well as I do.*

"We might all be alone right now," I said brightly, "but we have each other, right? And we're all safe and sound."

"I suppose there's something to that," Stephen said. "Although exactly what we're safe *from*, I still don't completely understand."

"All you have to know," I said, "is that a lot of things go on in this big world of ours. And people who are different are not necessarily crazy."

I knew that Stephen still struggled with the idea, but he was learning. As wonderful as he was, it wasn't going to hurt him any to have a more tolerant outlook. As for me, I had finally accepted who and what I was. I didn't always feel comfortable with it, but I couldn't hide or suppress it anymore. I laughed out loud as I thought of hanging out a shingle: *Lily Evans: Egyptologist, Artist and Psychic.*

"What's so funny?" Katy grumbled.

"I'm just...happy," I replied with a smile. "After all, tomorrow's my birthday!"

"Yikes! That's right!" Katy exclaimed. "With everything that's been going on—"

"We haven't exactly had time to—" Stephen chimed in.

"Well, you still have today. Off with the both of you. Stephen, take Katy to get a banana split, and then you can go shopping."

"And what are you going to do?" Katy asked.

"Oh, I don't know. Maybe I'll try to paint. It's been quite a while."

"That's a good idea," Katy said. "Okay, we'll give you some space. See you later!"

As soon as they left, I picked up the phone and dialed a number. "This is Lily," I said. "Is it done?"

"It's done," Derek's voice replied. "The whole congregation took part. I think Cal will be fine, and the portrait feels totally flat. Not the slightest vibration is left. Rose's power is destroyed forever."

"Thank God for that. You guys are awesome. I'm sorry I couldn't—"

"Don't say another word. You've been through enough. I just wish it wasn't insured so we could have burned the damn thing."

"I know, but Carolyn would've been responsible, and it could have ruined her. It's going back to Morrisville now. I talked to the curator at the Woodbine house. They're putting the picture in storage. No one liked it, and Carolyn is glad to have it off her hands."

"Aren't we all?" Derek replied heartily. "Okay, Lily. I'll talk to you later."

"Thanks, Derek. Thanks for everything."

As soon as I put the phone back in its cradle, it rang. Startled, I picked it back up. The voice at the other end made my heart swell. "Hello, dear. My, it seems like a long time since I've spoken to you."

"Mom! Mom, how are you?"

"I'm all right. I just had a delightful lunch. The nicest young man brought it. He reminded me of Stephen. Stephen has been so good about visiting. I do enjoy it. You'll be coming tomorrow, won't you?"

"I…um, of course I will."

"Good, good. I hope you like the present I picked out for you. I'm sorry I couldn't do a cake this year. Remember the ones you had growing up? You always wanted ballerinas and fairies, until I had to start putting sphinxes and pyramids on them. Well, I'm sure you'll get a cake from somewhere. There are so many good bakeries in town."

"I'll get one, don't worry." I choked back tears. "But it will never be as good as yours. I can't wait to see you, Mom."

"I'm looking forward to it. Come whenever you like, dear. Goodbye now."

Of all the strange things that had happened, that was the least expected. My mother had called me for the very first time since she'd gone into the hospital, and she sounded perfectly normal. I knew I shouldn't get my hopes up too high, but it had to be a good sign.

I got up in a kind of daze and went over to kneel by Cleocatra's basket. "Cleo, Mom has asked to see me! She's getting better. What a birthday present!"

I sat back on my heels and stared off into space. It was almost impossible to believe what the past two weeks had brought. In spite of all the terror and uncertainty, one thing had become clear to me: I was no longer trapped in that pink velvet box. The lid had come off, and the dancer was going on. I was entering a new stage of my life. The threshold guardian might not have been benign, but I had crossed the bridge anyway. And I was proud.

A *hiss* from Cleocatra interrupted my thoughts.

"No, no." I scratched her under the chin. "We're celebrating now, Cleo. We're okay."

A louder *hiss* clearly showed that she disagreed with me.

What could be wrong? I looked about nervously.

Then the doorbell rang.

Cleocatra stared at me fixedly, but she didn't move.

"Well, I'm going to get it. I'm not running away anymore." Still, my hand trembled a little bit as I prepared to open it. *How much can one heart take?*

"Hello, Lily."

Apparently, no more. My knees went weak, and I could only stare like an idiot. *Can this really be happening?*

"Happy birthday, love," Kent said.

Message from the Author

Dear Reader:

It was great having you along on Lily's latest adventure. I hope that you enjoyed yourself. It gave her strength to know that people were pulling for her. She might not have made it through the last battle with Rose if it weren't for you!

Being different can be very hard. Everyone wants to be accepted and valued for who they are. Sometimes it seems that the only way to do that is to be "normal." But we all know that there's no such thing.

Lily is learning to understand and believe in herself. It may not be psychic abilities that we have to come to terms with, but there are many challenges that face us each day. It takes real courage to step outside of our comfort zones and tackle something new. But only by doing so can we grow as human beings. Even if it hurts, hopefully from that pain we gain more strength of character and a greater appreciation of the world's diversity. And we might just find something more beautiful than we ever dreamed of.

Thank you all so much, and I'll be waiting for you in *Storm and Shadow*.

Love,

Susan

About the Author

Susan Jane McLeod has been writing since she was seven years old. At age eleven, she won a countywide essay contest, and her professional career was launched. By the time she was nineteen, her poetry had appeared in several magazines, including *American Girl* and *Seventeen*.

She also won an honorable mention in *The Writer*.

Susan grew up in Rochester, New York, with her three sisters and one brother. In her early thirties, she was diagnosed with ovarian cancer and given a 50/50 chance to live. She survived only to have the cancer recur, necessitating more surgery and an aggressive course of chemotherapy. Today she is cancer free.

The best job she's ever had was managing a bookstore, surrounded by her passion: literature.

Susan has published several short stories and two novels. The first, *Soul and Shadow*, is an award-winning paranormal historical romance. The second, *Fire and Shadow*, is classified as paranormal suspense. Both have garnered impressive reviews.

Susan believes strongly in several causes and has raised money for the American Cancer Society, Foodlink, and the House of Mercy homeless shelter.

She still resides in Rochester and will always call it home. Contact her at www.susanjmcleod.com or www.facebook.com/SusanJMcLeodAuthor

IMAJIN BOOKS

Quality fiction beyond your wildest dreams

For your next ebook or paperback purchase, please visit:

www.imajinbooks.com

www.facebook.com/imajinbooks

twitter.com/imajinbooks

www.ingramcontent.com/pod-product-compliance
Lightning Source LLC
Chambersburg PA
CBHW060423260626
47161CB00005B/1759